NIKOLAI

BASED ON THE FILM OF THE SAME TITLE

BILL MYERS ★

NIKOLAI

Marshall Pickering

First published in Great Britain in 1989 by Marshall Morgan and Scott
Reprinted in 1991 by
Marshall Pickering an imprint of
HarperCollinsReligious
Part of HarperCollins Publishers
77-85 Fulham Palace Road, London W6 8JB

Printed and bound in Great Britain by HarperCollins Manufacturing, Glasgow

A catalogue record for this book is available from the British Library

The film 'Nikolai' is available for rental
on 16mm and video from:
International Films,
235 Shaftesbury Avenue, London, and Gateway Films Inc.
2030 Wentz Church Road, Box A, Lansdale PA 19446, USA

Contents

For Mom and Dad:

''Train a child in the way he should go,
and when he is old he will not turn from it''
(Proverbs 22:6 NIV).

Thanks.

Foreword

Not long ago, Soviet citizens were surprised by a remarkable television program entitled "Response." The program was shown at about seven o'clock, a time when many people watch television. The viewers were invited to ask questions about democracy and human rights via a special telephone line. In the past such a thing was unthinkable, therefore many people were still very cautious and in many cases they did not give their names. The answers from the "experts" were a bit of a disappointment though. Obviously, they were not used to so much openness either!

Yet despite this example of the dramatic changes that seem to be taking place in the Soviet Union today because of "glasnost" (openness), it is still very important for each of us to remember that Christians there continue to be in great need of Bibles and our prayers and encouragement. "Openness" is nice, but we must not lose sight of reality.

That's why I'm grateful for a book like *Nikolai*. Through the life of this young Russian Christian we're reminded of the freedoms we take for granted, and challenged to make the most of those freedoms. But perhaps most importantly, this book causes us to more greatly value God's Word — the Bible — because it makes us aware that the time we live in and the time our children *will* live in is determined by our attitude towards the Bible.

My prayer is that *Nikolai* will not only cause you to cherish your Bible more, but also move you to aggressive prayer and active involvement in the other half of the world where Christians suffer daily for their faith. The opportunities are there, and we must take advantage of them!

In the battle together,

Brother Andrew

Chapter One

Papa knew the meeting was going to be dangerous. Course he never said anything — he never does. But you don't have to be a nuclear scientist to figure out when something's about to happen. I mean he can be as stone-faced as the best of us (a little trick we all learn as kids), but it's the little things that give him away. Like when he's just a little too interested in my day at school, or just a little too keen on Mama's borscht, or chuckles just a little too long over Pyotr's childishness.

But you can really tell something's about to happen when we're all in the family room (which is where Mama and Papa also sleep) and Papa just sits there watching me and Pyotr do our homework. That's it, that's all we do, just our homework. But he keeps on watching. He pretends to be reading or something but I can always tell.

There's just something different about him on those evenings; something, I don't know . . . softer. Once or twice I've even caught him touching the corner of his eyes. Those are the times we know something is about to happen.

There was another clue that the meeting was going to be dangerous. Because we are Unregistered Baptists all our services are forbidden. That means we have to secretly meet in each other's homes. At least, that's the idea. But for the past year or so the ''secret'' part has become kind of a joke. It seems like every time we showed up on a Sunday morning or weeknight the KGB was already there waiting for us. After a while we were all getting pretty tired of the arrests and fines and job demotions so we changed the meetings. We began meeting in a different apartment every week. That was pretty smart and worked real well . . . for about a month. But pretty soon, "surprise," there they were again — all scowls and once again passing out citations.

So, for the past few months we've begun to meet in the woods outside my town. It's a long walk and since the sun doesn't rise till 9:30 in the winter most of that journey is made in the dark. But that's okay. It's kinda interesting listening to the crunching of the snow under our boots and watching it sparkle up ahead in the moonlight. It's also fun comparing the ice cakes on the scarves we've been breathing through.

What is not fun is having to drag Pyotr along in the sled. He can be such a nuisance sometimes, always playing at being the "baby of the family." I can see right through his game but, for some reason, Mama and Papa can't. Maybe it has something to do with losing little Natasha last year. I don't know. But they sure dote and make a fuss over him, even though everyone can see he's playing it for all it's worth. Being the oldest isn't as much fun as you might think. Anyway, the snow is gone now and Mama promises that Pyotr will be old enough by next winter to walk all the way on his own. He'd better be.

But back to our meeting. First of all it was scheduled for a Wednesday. Nothing too unusual. And it was only for men. Again, nothing too strange. But what really made it interesting was that Papa wouldn't tell anyone where it was going to be. Instead the key leaders came to the tram station two hours before the meeting. Only then did he tell them the location. And, once they knew, they were to go and only tell those they trusted.

Now I suppose this sounds a little strange but you

have to keep in mind that everyone knows there's a KGB informer among us. Someone is being paid extra money and given special privileges for telling the KGB about our meetings. Papa wasn't hoping this would stop them, he was just hoping it would slow them down a little. Papa lives a lot on hope. Sometimes he's right. Sometimes not.

Oh, there was one other thing that made this men's meeting so special. For the very first time Papa let me come along.

* * *

We are the second or third ones to arrive at Ivan Krylov's apartment. As far as apartments go, it's pretty much like all the others. Two rooms — the bedroom for his mother, father and older brother, and the living room for him and his wife, and their two kids. Then of course they have to share the toilet and kitchen with another family.

Like everyone else they dream of having an apartment all to themselves. In fact I'm sure they applied for one before they even got married. But to get your own apartment a lot of times you have to know someone that owes you a favor or you have to pay a bribe or lie on your application. By lying you would say things like your mother and father really hate your wife; things like that. Of course, no one in our church would lie or pay the bribes, but if everyone else in our town is doing it I sometimes wonder what the big deal is. But, even if someone does lie or pay, they still have to do what we all have to do — they have to wait. Sometimes for years. But that's okay. Waiting is one thing we've all become experts at.

One by one the other members keep showing up — Dimitri Kozlov, Vladimir Ponomaryov, Mikhail Kanevski, all of the old standbys. Of course they don't all arrive at once. Instead they gradually trickle in over a couple of hours so they don't attract attention.

Suddenly there's a loud knock at the door. Because it's so much louder than the other knocks everyone is sure it's the KGB. But not Papa. Instead he quickly crosses to the door, throws it open and there, standing to greet him, to everyone's amazement, is a Westerner . . . an Englishman.

* * *

Peter Blackmore is a nice enough man. And even though he had taken great pains to make sure he wasn't being followed every one of us finds it hard to relax. Because, you see, your version of care and our version are often two different things. I can't tell you how many stories I've heard of Westerners (especially Americans) who just take a taxi right up to our apartments. More than one of Papa's friends has been rewarded with a KGB house search immediately after a Westerner's "careful" visit.

Then there is clothing. Dr. Blackmore did his best to dress in the dark solemn colors we wear for winter and early spring. But you just can't hide Western clothing from our eyes, especially when everybody wants to own some. I mean, you probably already know that your Levi jeans sell for about 200 roubles on our black market. That's way over a month's wages for most of us!

Whenever I visit Sasha, my cousin in Moscow, we have great fun riding the underground Metro and picking out the tourists. Some of you try so hard to look like us but I'm afraid there's always something to give you away. Like I said, it's usually in your clothes. But if for some reason we can't tell by that, we can always tell by your eyes. They're so, I don't know . . . open. I mean it's so easy to see what you're thinking. Real Russians look straight ahead and never show any expression, at least to strangers. But you people — I don't know, it's hard to explain.

Then there's the way you're always so quick to smile. Don't get me wrong; we like to laugh as much as the next person, but only with people we trust. You seem to grin and laugh with people that are almost perfect strangers.

And finally, there's the way you talk — not your language or your accent but your volume. We very seldom speak much above a whisper, yet you seem to speak as if you don't care who could be listening.

The best time we ever had over discovering a tourist was the American (or maybe he was English) who was dressed and who acted almost exactly like us. I mean he had everything down — the boots, the wool pants, the coat, the fur hat that the grown-ups wear in winter. He even carried that bored look of someone who's had too much of riding the Metro. He had us down to the tiniest detail except for one small matter . . . he was wearing his nice Russian fur hat backwards! Maybe someone told him. Maybe someone didn't. As I said, we Russians do like to laugh.

But back to the meeting. At first, things are going along just fine. We sing a few hymns and then some of the people stand and quietly speak of the Lord's goodness to them. Then we hit our first snag. Ivan Krylov is asked to open us up in prayer. Now I have nothing against praying but whenever Ivan gets the floor I know we're in for a long one. I don't know if you have Believers like this but it's as if he has to remind the Lord of all the hundred and one things that I'm sure the Lord already knows. He just goes on and on with, "and Lord, you know this and Lord you know that." It's more like he's preaching a sermon than praying a prayer. And it can really be tiring since we always kneel or stand when we pray.

No one has ever spoken to him about it, but it's interesting that whenever we have hot food Papa is careful never to ask him to say the blessing.

Eventually Ivan Krylov winds down and Dr. Blackmore begins to speak. I immediately like the man. Instead of telling us how sorry he feels for us and what great Christians we must all be, he just tells us about the latest events in the West and what a privilege he considers it to fellowship with us.

Things are going along quite nicely until suddenly Stepan Vasiliev, a few years older than me and a good quarter meter taller, spots movement outside the window that he's assigned to watch. He only says one word: "KGB." That's all it takes. The room flies into action.

Some grab the Bibles and quickly slip them under the floorboards in the corner. Others stuff pieces of hand-copied Scripture inside the sofa. All this as the rest of the men collect the song sheets and rearrange the room so it looks like we're just having tea. Meanwhile Mikhail, trying to disguise the panic in his voice, is calling out, "The Englishman, the Englishman."

Papa is quick to agree. "Yes, yes. Stepan take Dr. Blackmore out the back way."

As Stepan grabs the man's arm and leads him towards the door, Papa spins around and spots me. "Nikolai, you follow."

I try to protest but he's already cutting me off. "You're under age," he says. "It will be much worse if they find you here."

Again I try to argue but Papa is already directing his attention back to Dr. Blackmore who is trying to free himself from Stepan's grip. "We've done nothing illegal," Blackmore is arguing. "We've broken no laws."

If it were another time Papa may have burst out laughing. Instead he evenly explains, "What is legal and what is permissible are often very different, Dr. Blackmore."

Again Stepan tries to take him out the door and again the doctor resists. "I don't see—"

"Hurry!" Papa orders.

"Park Allegiance — 5:00 p.m., the day after tomorrow."

Papa doesn't understand. "What?"

"We will have Bibles for your group. Park Allegiance, 5:00 p.m., Wednesday."

There's a moment of silence as Papa searches the man's face, but there's no missing the good doctor's sincerity. At last Papa breaks into a grin and hoarsely says, "Thank you." Then, just to make sure he's got it right, he repeats, "5:00 p.m., Wednesday."

In the silence we hear the KGB enter the lift just a few stories below. Stepan wastes no more time. He knows if they don't move now there'll be no moving. He grabs the doctor's arm and forces him out the door.

"God be with you, my Brother," Papa calls after him as they head for the stairs.

I try to slink behind the door hoping with all the distraction that Papa has forgotten his orders to me. I should have known better. Immediately he searches me out and practically shouts, "GO!"

15

But I don't go, I can't go.

"Papa." I race to him and throw my arms around him hoping he'll understand, hoping he won't make me leave him. He understands alright. But he won't change his mind. I still remember the wet wool smell of his coat as he lets me hug him for just the briefest moment. Then he firmly pulls me away and looks me right in the eyes. There's no missing the glint of moisture around the corners.

"I will be fine," he answers. His voice is a little husky sounding. "We are in His care, are we not?"

There'll be no reasoning now; not when he brings up God. Papa's a good man but he can be terribly stubborn when it comes to God. Now, I'm not saying the Lord doesn't protect, but sometimes His version of protection and our version . . . well, they're not always the same. I want to say this. I want to say that I trust God but also that I don't. I want to run away but I also want to stay by Papa's side. I want to scream at him for taking too many chances and I want to apologize for all the times I've doubted. I want to say all these things but nothing comes out. All I can do is hug him again, hoping he'll understand. But he doesn't. Or maybe he does. In any case he's again peeling my arms away.

And then he gives me the strangest look I have ever seen. I can't explain it exactly but it's almost as if he were pleading — as if he were begging me not to show weakness — as if he somehow needed my strength so he could hang on to his. It lasts only a moment but it makes my whole body go cold. I'll never forget it.

I'm sure he doesn't touch me. It's almost as if it's the look itself that throws me backwards. In any case I find myself stumbling away and then turning and starting to race down the hall. I barely reach the steps when I hear the lift jolt to a stop and the door being pushed open, but I don't turn around.

I race through the courtyard, tears burning my eyes. But I will not stop. I can not stop.

Fathers are supposed to be strong; we're supposed to need their help, they're not supposed to need ours. But I know what I saw in his eyes. It lasted only a moment but I know what I saw.

* * *

Later, at home, I carefully go over every detail with Mama — several times. Who was there, what Dr. Blackmore said, Papa's last words, how many I heard getting out of the lift. But I do not tell her about Papa's eyes. How can I? How could she bear it? Papa's always been in charge, he's always been our rock. To have him afraid, to have him actually need help . . . that would be more than she could bear.

* * *

Papa's look haunts me all night. It makes no difference where I stare, I just keep on seeing it. Even when I fall asleep, I keep seeing it. I keep seeing his eyes.

Chapter Two

There's something else about my father I think you should know. I've always loved him and he's always loved me. But lately, for some reason, things have started to change between us. I can't put my finger on it exactly but it seems like he's tougher, like he's not as kind. I don't see him being that way with Pyotr or Mama; only with me. Like the time I was buying Mama some nice flowers at the market.

They were beautiful carnations and, though they cost nearly a rouble apiece, I thought two or three would be wonderful for the table. When I got to the counter to pay and discovered I was several kopecks short, Papa didn't volunteer to help. He always had in the past. In fact sometimes he'd offer to pay for the whole gift. But this time he said I'd have to go back and return one of them. I didn't think much about it then but, like I said, this sort of thing seems to be happening more and more.

The time it hurt the most was about three months ago on the tram. It was one of those cold days where everyone's breath had iced up the inside of the windows, making those wonderful frost patterns. In fact it was so thick that if you weren't lucky enough to sit by a window where you could scrape off a little peephole, you really couldn't tell where you were.

Anyway, Pyotr was crowded in real close to Papa and the two were playing a little game where Pyotr pretended to steal one of Papa's coat buttons. It was a game Papa and I had originally invented and since there was nothing else to do I thought I'd join in. I tried it once or twice but Papa wouldn't pay any attention. Finally, after the third time, he took my hand and gently set it at my side. I looked at him, not understanding and again reached for his button. Again he took my hand and put it at my side. But this time he firmly held it, making it clear that I could not play.

"Be strong," he said.

I looked at him puzzled. He gently patted my hand and repeated himself. "Be strong." And then, without missing a beat, he turned and continued to play with Pyotr.

I didn't understand it then and I don't understand it now, but it always makes me sad when I think about it. I know we'll never play the game again.

*　　*　　*

Mama's oats are a little more watery than usual but I know this is not the morning to complain. She has been up most of the night, calling friends, asking them to pray, and doing a lot of praying herself. But Papa never came home.

Now Pyotr is gulping down his food like there's no tomorrow and complaining between bites about how unfair it all is; that Papa has done nothing wrong. Mama listens with half an ear but not much more.

Mornings have always been hectic for her — fixing breakfast at 6:45, getting Papa off to the tram by 7:20, getting us off to school by 7:30. Then there is the constant juggling in sharing the toilet with the Semyonovs and the Rusnaks, and finally getting herself to work by 8:00. It wouldn't be so hard if she and Papa both didn't have to work on the other side of town, but since the government tells us where we must live she has no choice.

Her days aren't much better than her mornings. After putting in a full day at the textile mill she has to spend two hours, three or four times a week, going to different shops until she gets what she needs to come home and prepare supper.

You'd hate our shops. We all do. First, they never have what you need. That's why Mama has to shop so much. Sometimes she has to go to three or four stores just to find milk! And when she finally finds one that has what she needs she has to wait in line forever just to tell the clerk behind the counter what she wants. The clerk then writes down the name of the item and how much it costs on a slip of paper. You have to take that piece of paper and go stand in another long line to pay the cashier. Once the cashier gets your money, she stamps the receipt and you have to go back to that first line and wait all over again until you can hand it to the clerk. Finally she gives you the item . . . if they still have it!

You can see why Mama doesn't always have so much energy. And this morning, since she hasn't slept, it's even tougher for her. But she still manages to win in the ongoing war to get Pyotr to button his coat and put on his hat.

I try to suggest that it might be better if we all stayed home but she will hear none of it. Instead she reminds me of the swimming tryouts that afternoon, the ones I've been working so hard for. And then, when she's sure Pyotr's not paying attention, she lowers her voice and finally says what's on both of our minds:

"It's not as if this is the first time such a thing has happened."

I glance down, saying nothing. She continues. "Each

time has not the good Lord remained faithful — has He not protected us?''

Again I say nothing but she insists on some sort of answer. ''Well?''

I know what I have to do. I know I have to smile and play the part. Even though I don't feel like it, even though I'm scared to death that something terrible is going to happen to Papa, I know what Mama expects. So I raise my head and give her a little nod.

And that's all she needs. For the briefest moment her face lights up and all the fear seems to disappear. I feel a little guilty faking it like that but I know it's something she needs. I even manage to squeeze out a little smile. She returns it (though I'm sure it's just as forced). Then as if she's afraid we'll find out what we're both really thinking, she spins me around and gives me a playful shove towards the door.

''Scoot,'' she says, ''or you'll be late for school.''

*   *   *

The walk to school is usually about 20 minutes of non-stop boredom. Especially now, when everything is still brown from the winter and mushy from the melted snow. To top it off, everywhere you look there are these monotonous twelve-story buildings we all live in. Each one is the same height, the same length, the same muddy orange — each one has the same torn screens, the same crying children, the same little balconies. The only thing different is the type of laundry strung across the balconies — and sometimes even that's the same.

Then, of course, there's Pyotr's motor mouth. He's always got something to chatter on about and I'm afraid this morning's no different. Fortunately he's already asked Mama his million and one questions about Papa.

So all I have to put up with is, "Can I stay and watch your tryouts? What if I just stand way off in the corner? Please? What if I don't say anything? What if I wear a disguise so no one would recognize me?"

Of course he already knows the answer to these questions so I don't waste the air to speak.

I don't know what it is but lately it seems like all he wants to do is hang around me. To be honest, it's getting pretty embarrassing. I mean, who wants their little brother tagging along everywhere. Don't get me wrong, I still keep an eye on him and help him out if he runs into trouble — but playing baby-sitter 24 hours a day is not my idea of a good time.

Luckily it isn't too long before he spots some of his friends and races on ahead shouting, "Sasha, Volodya . . . guess what happened?"

To him it's just a game. I shake my head and sigh. Ah, to be young again.

I take advantage of the opportunity and go a slightly different route — the one I take when I want to think, the one that leads through the stand of oak and birch trees, past the old Orthodox Church — the one that takes me to Babushka's grave.

Babushka, or Grandmother as you would say, was a terrific lady. She had her problems, especially towards the end before she died, but basically she was a lot of fun. We had these little secrets and jokes we used to play on Mama and Papa. Probably the best was the time she snuck me into her church to get baptized — just in case Mama and Papa's dedication of me as a baby didn't take.

We never talked much about it, but I know it broke Babushka's heart when Mama left the Orthodox Church to marry Papa and become a Baptist. You see, for 1,000 years now, the Orthodox Church has been Russia's official Church. (I'm sure you've seen their gold domes and spires in history books and stuff.) We Baptists didn't come along until a lot later. In fact even today we're still looked upon as being real strange — you know, as foreigners, and something to be suspicious of. But that's okay. We have our doubts about the Orthodox too.

First of all Mama and Papa say the church is riddled with spies. I guess that could be, since the government has such tight control over them and their seminaries and everything. But all I see are little old ladies who don't look a whole lot like KGB to me. I suppose some of the young people, who are starting to come more and more often, could be spies, but they all seem pretty sincere when they talk about looking for their "roots," and trying to find out who they are.

Mama and Papa's biggest worry is that the Orthodox Church is supposed to be caught up in a bunch of tradition — you know the worshiping of idols and saints and things like that. They say they really don't have any kind of "living faith" in Jesus Christ.

I don't know about all that but I do know they're really different. I mean from the moment you walk in the gates you know you're not at one of our meeting places. First of all there's all those gold and painted domes I mentioned. But that's only on the outside. When you get on the inside your eyes practically pop out at all the gold and candles and statues and stuff.

Everywhere you look there are pictures (icons they're called) of different saints and different people in the Bible. Babushka said that all these icons are around to make you feel like you're being surrounded by Scripture. It's supposed to be especially helpful to the older people who never learned to read. To them these pictures are like the words of Scripture. She used to call them, "Windows to Heaven," and claimed that no one was really worshiping them but that they were just using them to help focus better on some section of the Bible or on Jesus.

It seemed to make sense, although sometimes I wonder if kissing them and all that isn't really getting a little carried away. Still, after he's read a real moving passage in the Bible, I've seen Papa quietly kiss it. Maybe there's not that much difference.

Oh, I forgot to mention about the incense and the fact that there aren't any pews. You just stand the whole service and mostly sing and pray something called the "liturgy." Actually it's kinda neat, especially the way the people get into it. A lot of times Babushka would fast before she went so her mind would really be clear. And between the incense, and the music, and the voices, and the icons, I could see where you could really lose yourself in worship. If you ask me, I think that might be okay — I mean if it's focused on God and everything. But then again, I'm just a kid. Maybe when I get older I'll understand what's supposed to be so wrong with it.

By now I've arrived at the church's gate. I give it a pull but since it's not a Sunday or a special feast day it's locked. So I cross around the back to the cemetery and lean my head against the red iron bars of the fence. They're kind of chilly but my stocking hat, my favorite that has "Adidas" written on it, seems to absorb most of the cold.

Way off in the middle, almost out of sight, is Babushka's gravestone. Sometimes, especially in late afternoon, the light will hit it just right and you can see her picture reflecting in the sun. But of course it's too early right now.

She was the closest. In all the years she lived with us, before the pneumonia, I knew that she understood me the best. In fact she was the one who first noticed my interest in writing, and she's the one who looked and looked until she finally found and bought me a copy of Leo Tolstoy's *Anna Karenina*. Of course there are lots of parts in it I don't understand but I'm not about to skip a single word. And it is true, he does seem to go on and on and on, but there are lots of sections that are very good. Papa says Tolstoy had a gift to capture the Russian soul with words. Someday, I'd like to be able to do the same. I know it's a long way off, but they say it doesn't hurt to dream.

Usually when I'm here at the fence or inside, I have nice long talks with Babushka. Today I really don't have anything to say. I just want to be close. Oh, I suppose I could rattle on about something but the words would have no meaning because inside, where I really live, I have no feeling. Not today. Today, all I have is numbness . . .

*   *   *

At school Stepan (or Stenik as his friends call him) catches my eye and we head down the hall towards our classes together. He quietly speaks making sure no one hears. ''The others,'' he says, ''they were fined heavily and released early this morning.''

My heart sinks.

Of course I'm happy for him; both his father and uncle were at the meeting. But at the same time I can't help but feel a little angry. After all Papa is a good man — as good if not better than Stenik's father. Why didn't God release him? Of course, I can't say this. I'm embarrassed enough to even be thinking it.

Stenik asks if we've heard any word on Papa.

I shake my head.

He seems to understand and instead of giving me a big long speech on how I should trust God, or on how we should expect persecution, all he says is, "I'm sorry."

I like that.

Chapter Three

We have Galina Ivanovna third period on Mondays, Wednesdays and Fridays. And even though I'm not too crazy about science, her class is still my favorite. I think it has something to do with the way she teaches.

You see normally, ever since kindergarten, we've been taught to memorize our lessons — you know facts, figures, that sort of thing. And then, when we're called, we're supposed to be able to recite them back to the teachers exactly the way we learned them. "Repetition is the Mother of Knowledge," they say.

But not in Galina Ivanovna's class. Instead, she asks questions that the textbooks haven't even covered. "I want you to think on your own," she says. "If I wanted to train parrots, I'd be a zoo keeper." At first it's kind of scary, and a lot of the kids don't like it. But once you get the hang of it, thinking on your own is fun.

For the past couple of weeks we've been working on our science projects and demonstrating them to the class. Mine is on "Behavior Modification." At first I was just going to make a bunch of charts and diagrams. But then, out of the blue, Galina Ivanovna brought in this incredible bunny for me to train. I call him (I think it's a him) Vanya. And the whole class really loves him.

Anyway, that's the kind of teacher she is. She makes you think on your own, and a lot of times that's not so easy, but she's always there to help and offer suggestions. She makes you work, sure — but at the same time, underneath it all, you know she really cares.

My family has known her family for years. In fact they even used to go to our church, but that was a long time ago — before they took her brother.

Now she is a member of the Communist Party. Of course this means she had to take a special oath of allegiance to the Party and the government. We, as Christians, could never take that oath. She also has to go to special classes on Marx or Lenin or Communism once a week. Also, she has to donate certain of her free days for special work projects.

I know this sounds like a lot but, other than having to deny God, the benefits seem pretty much worth it.

For one, she gets to teach. As a Christian she would never get a job that lets her be around so many people. In fact Papa used to be a taxi driver before they fired him. (I think they caught him witnessing to a KGB guy or something.)

Then there's the special stores she gets to shop in that the rest of us aren't even allowed to go into. In fact, at the Gum shopping mall in Moscow, the Party members get a whole floor to themselves.

And finally, because she is a Party member, Galina Ivanovna will be the first one the authorities remember when it comes to promotions and special privileges.

Now none of these may seem like much by themselves but in a system where the only way you can get ahead is through bribes and special privileges you can see where it can start to add up.

Oh, I almost forgot. The other reason I like Galina Ivanovna's class has to do with Vera Vladimirovna. I don't know when it first started, but lately I've caught her stealing looks at me more and more often. I'd be lying if I said it didn't make me feel good. I mean, every time I glance over my shoulder, there she is staring away. Of course she pretends she isn't but it only takes a couple of times before a guy starts to figure out what's really happening. Also, it doesn't hurt that she happens to be about the best-looking girl in my class!

There are only two things that worry me. The first is Viktor Sergeevich. The guy's about twice my size, real athletic, and real strong. The problem is he's been going with Vera for about three months now. That's problem one. The good news is they broke up early last week and everybody in the school knows about the split. Well, almost everyone. Viktor, who is not always so bright, still hasn't got the message. That's problem two.

Anyway, for the past few days I've been trying to work up the courage to ask if I can sit with her at lunch. Now don't get me wrong, it's not like I'm scared of her or anything like that. It's just, well, when a guy makes this sort of a move he doesn't want to come off sounding like some sort of goon. So last week I spent a couple of days practicing. You know, choosing the right words, making sure my voice stayed cool and steady, and just overall trying to be relaxed. Anyway by Monday I knew I was ready.

Everything started off perfect. At least two different times I caught her looking at me. So, when the bell finally rang, I knew the time had come. It was now or never. I scooped up my books as nonchalantly as possible, ran the speech in my head one last time, and sauntered on over to her desk. Things couldn't have been better. She was actually staying behind to chat with a friend, almost as if she knew what I was going to do. (It kind of makes you wonder.)

Anyway, the first sign of a problem came when I noticed I couldn't swallow; it wasn't that I couldn't swallow, it was that I had nothing to swallow. My mouth was as dry as cotton. But that was okay — I figured at least I wouldn't spit on her. But when I finally got there and opened my mouth, nothing came out. I couldn't believe it. I quickly cleared my throat and tried again. Of course by this time her friend had signaled her and they had both turned around to welcome me.

"Oh, hi, Kolya," she said. (Kolya is what my friends call me for short.)

I smiled stupidly.

"Is there something you want?" she prompted.

I opened my mouth but again there was nothing. Again I smiled.

She smiled back, a little puzzled.

Again I cleared my throat and again there was nothing . . . except a raspy little squeak.

She kept smiling but I could see it was slowly turning to one of those smiles you give to an injured puppy or something. Her friend was glancing to the ground trying not to laugh.

"Is everything alright?" she ventured.

I coughed.

She threw a concerned look to her friend. I could tell she was beginning to wonder if maybe she had made some sort of terrible mistake. Maybe she had wasted all this time liking some sort of mental reject. I knew it was a time for desperate measures and, thanks to my quick thinking, I was able to find an immediate solution.

Behind them on the bulletin board was a poster that a student had brought in earlier that year, showing three or four of our beloved cosmonauts. Having lost a thumbtack, one of its corners now hung loose, waving in the breeze from the hallway.

"Look at this," I croaked, breaking past them to the board. "Someone should have fixed this long ago." I pulled down the corner, found another tack, and stuck it back to the board.

"There," I said, giving it a little tap.

They smiled.

"Well, I guess I'll see you tomorrow."

They kept smiling.

With that I coughed slightly, turned, and slunk on into the hallway. It was not my best attempt and I could feel their stares as I disappeared around the corner. My only hope was she might like guys who cared about neatness.

So here it is Wednesday. Viktor is up front demonstrating his project. Like two or three other kids in class he's made a model of the solar system. Of course Earth's blue, of course Mars is red, and of course Saturn's got rings. But he still has to point all this out to us. As he keeps droning on I try resisting the temptation to glance over my shoulder. At first I'm able to, but pretty soon I know I have to take a peek. I do and sure enough, there's Vera, her eyes suddenly darting away from me, pretending she wasn't staring. There's still hope.

Viktor is now showing us how each of his planets revolve around a yellow styrofoam ball that's supposed to be the sun. But one of the planets, I think it's Mercury, seems to be stuck. He gives it a pull but nothing happens. The kids snicker. He tries again — still nothing.

I figure this is as good a time as any to double-check on Vera, you know just to make sure her looking at me wasn't an accident. I give her another glance, but this time when she looks away she breaks into a shy little grin. Poor girl. I can tell she's really embarrassed. I mean it must be terrible to like someone as much as she seems to like me. Once again I make up my mind — if not for me, at least for her. I'll definitely ask her about lunch.

Suddenly everyone breaks out in laughter and I turn back to see Viktor's sun exploding into a million pieces in his hands. Like I said, he's strong but not always too bright.

The bell rings and Galina Ivanovna is quickly on her feet in front of the class. "Grigori, Lidia, Elena," she says, "you'll be demonstrating your projects Friday."

Normally we enter and leave our classroom in single file — girls first, then boys. But today I notice Viktor is pushing a couple of kids aside and heading directly for Vera's desk. It's pretty obvious he's angry about something. Now, I still plan on talking to Vera but I figure it would be healthier to wait a minute or two.

I can't hear what they're saying but he seems to be making some kind of demand.

She shakes her head. Again, he says something and again, she shakes her head. But this time she glances up to me for just the tiniest of seconds. That's all it takes. Viktor spots it. Of course I pretend to be gathering my books but I'm really asking God to take special interest in my protection. Viktor turns and says something else to her and then storms off.

I'll be giving him a wider berth these next few days.

Anyway, the room's practically empty now and I know the time has come; it's now or never. I make my move, but before I have a chance to say anything she looks up with the cutest smile I've ever seen in my life and says, "Good luck with the swimming tryouts, Kolya. I hope you make the team."

I'm speechless. Not only has she been watching but she's obviously been doing some research too. She keeps smiling.

"Thanks," I finally croak.

She nods and keeps smiling. We stand a moment until I suddenly remember my purpose for being there. "I'm going to lunch in a minute," I hear myself say. "Can I catch up with you?"

"I'll save you a place."

Again she flashes me that beautiful grin, and before I can answer she turns and glides into the hallway out of sight. I stand another moment, trying to take it all in, trying to comprehend how one person can have such good fortune.

Eventually I come to and spot Vanya in his cage at the back of the room. His food tray is empty so I cross over to feed him.

He's a bunny with long ears that reach all the way back to his hind legs. And he's so soft that if you weren't a guy you'd just want to squash him and hug him and bury your face into his fur. Of course I don't. Instead I give him a carrot which he immediately starts gnawing down. It's only then that I notice our teacher, Galina Ivanovna, standing a few feet beside me, filling up one of the beakers of another experiment.

"He's a wonderful project," she says. "You're really making progress with him."

I always like the kindness in her voice, but I'm not sure what to do with a compliment like that so I just nod and give Vanya another carrot. Galina Ivanovna clears her throat. I shift my weight to the other foot. After another moment she finally speaks, saying what we both know she's been thinking all along. "I am sorry to hear of your father."

I nod, not at all surprised about how fast the word has traveled.

"How is your mother taking it?"

"You know Mama," I say, clearing my throat. "She just smiles and says such things are expected."

She nods and we stand there for another long moment. Only Vanya's chomping breaks the silence. I'm beginning to look for a graceful way to leave.

"It doesn't have to be that way Kolya, not for you," she says.

I keep looking at Vanya. There's no doubt in my mind what Galina Ivanovna's getting at. I wish I'd already left but I didn't so now all I can do is keep quiet and hope she'll move on to something else.

She tries again — this time sounding a little more official. "I have entered your project to represent our school at the State Science Fair."

What? The State Science Fair! Me? Are such things possible? She smiles at the excitement that I've let slip onto my face.

"Of course they asked me if you were a member of the Young Pioneers."

Here it comes. I take in a deep breath. She continues.

"I had to say no, but assured them you would join as soon as possible."

There it is! I knew the news was too good to be true; there had to be a catch. The Young Pioneers is a group we're all expected to join at about nine years old. It's quite a step in each of our lives. In fact you can always depend on the initiation ceremony to be full of lots of fanfare, banners and a few teary-eyed children.

It usually starts off with the kids marching around for a while and listening to speeches about the privilege of being a Young Pioneer. You know, how it's the first step in officially contributing to our great country, and how, like their parents, the kids will remember that day all of their lives. Then at last, when everyone's done, they finally get around to the oath which goes like this:

"I (fill in your own name), on entering the ranks of the All-Union Pioneer Organization named after Vladimir Ilyich Lenin, solemnly promise before my peers:

"To love my motherland deeply.

34

"To live, study, and fight as the great Lenin commanded and as the Communist Party teaches.

"And to always observe the laws of the Young Pioneers of the Soviet Union."

After the oath, the older children come and tie a red scarf around their necks. Then a wreath is placed on whatever memorial the town has of Lenin. And, finally, everyone is silent for a minute in memory of the man. It's a tremendous day of celebration and one that every nine-year-old takes part in. Well, almost every nine-year-old. As a Believer in Jesus Christ, I didn't.

Galina Ivanovna continues the pressure. "I gave them my word, Kolya."

I keep looking down. I know it's really not her fault. If you're a teacher it's very embarrassing to have a non-member in your class. She's embarrassed, her supervisor is embarrassed, his supervisor is embarrassed and so on up the ladder. I guess everyone is under a lot of pressure to try and make us take the oath — so to blame anyone, especially Galina Ivanovna, really isn't that fair.

You'd think after all these years I'd get used to it. But I haven't. It's still hard. It's hard when they show all those films making fun of Christians. When they make us stand in front of the class. When they claim that as Baptists we're a cult. When they say we're weak-minded. When everybody wants to argue with you and prove that there is no God.

I'll never forget the time in kindergarten when our teacher scientifically set out to prove to the class that God did not exist. She brought in two plants — both real healthy. She explained that she would take care of one and if there was a God she would let Him take care of the other.

She set the two plants up front on her desk, side by side, and kept them there for weeks. It was pretty hard to watch the one she watered and took care of grow and bloom while the one God was in charge of slowly dried up and died. Every day I went to class hoping it would get better. And every day when I saw it my heart fell a little lower. Even after it was completely dead the teacher kept it right beside her beautiful blooming plant for what seemed like forever. Of course all the kids understood this to be "scientific proof" that God didn't exist. And even though I knew it was a lie, even though I knew God had created the plant to live outside where there was rain, to this day I still see that dead, withered plant in my mind.

But we're not always such innocent victims. At least I'm not. It's very embarrassing for me to say this and up till now Babushka's the only one that's ever known. But there was a time back in fourth grade that we were told to stand up and shout and shake our fists at God. I wish I could say I refused and maybe, in a way, I did. I mean I stood and shook my fist but I really didn't shout. I opened my mouth and everything, but I didn't say anything.

Since then I've prayed a million times that Jesus would forgive me, and I hope maybe somehow He has.

But you know what I remember most about all of it was this one girl who refused to shake her fist. When the teacher noticed, she made us stop and demanded to know why the girl wasn't joining in. Was she a Jew? Was she a Christian? What?

The girl shook her head. She was none of those things. She knew there was no God, and that was the very thing that was so confusing to her. Since there was no God she just wasn't sure who she was shaking her fist at.

Papa uses that in his sermons from time to time and it always brings about a little chuckle. But I've always been bothered by the fact that this little girl, who didn't even know God, seemed to have more courage than me. I suppose this seems like a small thing, but to me it is not. It always stays there at the back of my mind.

"Why must you be so stubborn?" Galina Ivanovna is demanding. "Everyone else in the class has joined. Everyone else wears the red scarf . . ."

Vanya has finished the carrot and I slowly close the cage. I would give everything I have to get out of there — to leave and join Vera at lunch.

"Do you know what the other children say about you? They say you think you're too good to join; that you're better than the rest of them."

I can feel my ears starting to turn red.

"Is that what you think, Kolya? Is it?"

I shake my head. Fortunately I notice Vanya's little tin watering dish is empty. Here's something I can do. I open the cage and pick it up, brushing the straw out of it, being careful not to cut myself on its sharp, jagged edge.

"You are missing so much . . . When was the last time you participated in the music programs . . . hm? Or the weekend field trips . . . or, for that matter, any youth activity?"

I'm starting to get angry. She knows these answers better than me. As a non-member I can't participate in any of the Pioneer activities. I can't even go to the Pioneer Palaces where everyone meets after school. That's where you learn to build model airplanes that really fly, or study photography, or practice foreign languages, or, well you name it.

"And all because you won't join," she says. "Why, Kolya? Why do you continue to refuse? Why?"

Almost before I know it, I'm answering. I know I shouldn't but I can't help it. "To join I would have to deny God."

There, I've said it. I hope I didn't hurt her feelings but it had to be said.

She lets out a quiet sigh. "Kolya, you would not have to deny God."

Surely she doesn't think I'm that stupid. I know the real meaning of the oath when it says, "To live, study, and fight as the Communist Party teaches." I throw her a look.

"No," she insists. "I haven't."

I can't believe my ears. How is it possible? "But," I stutter, "everyone thinks that, that . . ."

"That I've turned my back on God?"

I can only nod.

"That's what they're supposed to think. And, on the outside, I have. I say what the Party tells me to say, I do what they tell me to do . . . But that's only on the outside. Inside, here," she points to her heart. "Here, where it really counts, I still believe, Kolya."

Are such things possible?

"I believe," she continues, "just as you. Yet I have full privileges."

Is this possible? Could Mama and Papa have overlooked something so obvious? But if it could be done, if we could have the best of both worlds . . . My mind starts to race with possibilities. Can this really be?

Part of me is saying, "No, this is a fairy tale, this is a trap." But there's the other part that's saying, "Yes! I've suspected it all along! There is a way out!"

"Kolyasha, I speak to you as a friend. Our families have known each other for years. Don't throw your life away . . . not on something this trivial."

I'm not sure what she means — my mind is still back

at what she said a minute before. But I notice a touch of anger creeping into her voice.

"Do you want to live like your father? Continually watched by the State . . . working at the most menial labor . . . barely able to support your family?"

This I understand. But she's got it wrong, all wrong. "That's all figured out," I explain. "I will attend the University of Moscow, I will become a writer, maybe a lawyer and help fellow – "

"What?" she interrupts. "Go to the University? You silly boy. They won't let you attend the University . . . any university."

It's my turn to interrupt, to explain that she doesn't have all the facts.

But she continues, not even hearing. "If you are not a member of the Young Pioneers or the Komsomol, your education will stop next year." She lowers her voice. "They will see to it that you go no further. You will not pass your oral exams. The only thing awaiting you will be vocational school — plumbing, carpentry . . . Is that what you want, Kolya?"

I know my mouth is open; I know she's gotten inside and is reading all my thoughts but there is nothing I can do. I feel Vanya's watering tin starting to twist in my hands but I don't look down.

"You will be of help to no one. All of your intelligence, all of your hard work, all of your studies . . . they will be in vain, Nikolai."

I can only stare into Vanya's cage. There's a heaviness in my chest. It's becoming difficult to breathe. Suddenly I feel her hand on my shoulder. I want to slap it away, to shove her to the floor, but I can't move.

"That is why it is so important. Your entire future is at stake."

I don't know how long we stand. I don't know what

else she says. All I can hear is my heart pounding in my ears. Finally, I feel her hand leave my shoulder and hear: ''Think about it, will you please? Just . . . think about it.''

She turns and I hear her heels click away as she heads back to her desk at the front.

I don't know what to do, where to go. I glance down at my hands. They are white from gripping Vanya's tin. They are white and bleeding.

Chapter Four

I concentrate hard on Lenin's reflection wavering on the surface of the pool. It comes from the bright red banner of his profile that hangs on the side wall. I inch my toes to the very edge of the platform and wait — every one of my muscles tenses and is ready to explode.

There's the whistle.

I leap for all I'm worth, right into the center of the reflected face. It's a good start and I feel myself shooting underwater at my best speed, but, as I surface, I start stroking too quickly. I'm exploding alright, but in too many directions. Nothing's smooth. Everything's disjointed. I am too angry. I have too much energy. I'm trying too hard and I know it. I feel more like I'm fighting at the water than pushing through it.

Of course I'm making progress but it's nothing like when Stenik and I practiced. I try to force myself to settle down, to lengthen my strokes. It's a struggle but gradually I'm able to make myself relax and slowly let my instincts start to take over. My strokes grow smoother, my follow-throughs longer. All those months of practice are starting to pay off. All those weeks of Stenik nagging and drilling at me to "concentrate, concentrate, concentrate" — finally they're starting to make a difference.

I've still got all this energy trying to break out from inside of me, but now I'm making it work for me, not against me. I even begin counting . . . "one, two, one, two . . ." I've finally got a pattern, I've finally fallen into the groove that we worked so long to establish. I catch a glimpse of the pool's wall as it comes into view. There are two, maybe three other swimmers ahead of me. "One, two, one, two." The wall looms into view and my timing couldn't be better as I tuck under and push off — harder than I ever remember pushing off before.

I wait until the last second, stretching for all I'm worth, until I surface and begin to stroke, "One, two, one, two . . ." I'm flying. Everything else is out of my mind. I'm on another planet. Here there is no hurt, there is no anger. I'm free. I'm free of Galina Ivanovna, I'm free of Papa, I'm free of God. "One, two, one, two . . ." I know by now I should start to feel it in my lungs, I should be hoping for the end, but I feel nothing — no pain, no burning — only freedom.

I glance to my sides. There's no other water breaking beside or ahead of me. I'm in the lead. The heat is mine. I'm nearly on the team.

"But you have to concentrate."

"Yes, but I'm nearly there."

"Concentrate."

"Of course, but—"

"CONCENTRATE!"

"One, two, one, two . . ."

For the briefest second I remember one of our family outings, just before Pyotr was born. Papa had me on his shoulders and we were running through a birch forest. We were just tall enough to be lost in the lower leaves and branches. Faster and faster we went, the leaves and dangling fronds crashing into our faces, but we didn't care, we were laughing too hard. Faster and faster. I could not see the sky, I could not see the ground. All I could see were leaves and fronds as I hung on for dear life, laughing and screaming all the way.

That's how it is now; no top, no bottom, just water.

I have no weight, I have no existence. I'm just floating — floating and flying, and nothing can touch me.

"But I have to concentrate."

"Yes, but you'll show them, you'll show them all."

"Concentrate!"

"Of course but—"

"CONCENTRATE!"

"One, two, one, two . . ."

And then, suddenly, I see Papa's expression in front of me. I try to shake it but it keeps coming back from different angles, closer and closer.

"One, two, one, two . . ."

And then his voice. "We are in His care are we not?"

"Concentrate!"

"One . . ."

"We are in His care—"

"Two . . ."

". . . Are we not?"

"CONCENTRATE!"

"ONE—"

His face is nearly on top of me. I feel myself starting to falter, my rhythm breaking up. The wall is only a few meters ahead. If I can just—

"WE ARE—"

"TWO—"

"IN HIS—"

"ONE—"

"CARE—"

"CONCENTRATE!"

"ARE WE—"

"ONE, ONE—"

It's gone, I'm lost. I feel myself starting to thrash, beating against the water. But suddenly, somehow, some way, my hand hits the wall. I pop my head up gasping for air. I look around . . . just as the second and third places touch the wall.

I've made it. Somehow I've won the heat! I look around and spot Stenik beaming above me, reaching out to take my hand.

"Congratulations," he says. "Welcome aboard."

"You think I made it?" I ask, still trying to catch my breath.

"No sweat — though I've seen better style from an ardvark." He grins and throws his towel around my neck. But something catches his eye and for the tiniest of moments the smile freezes.

I turn to see.

There, standing next to our coach is a tall, balding man with a white shirt and dark suit. He's speaking quietly to her as she jots something down on her clipboard. None of this should be of any concern except for one small detail — when they look up they're both staring right at me!

I start to ask Stenik who he is, what's going on, but before I get out the words I find myself flying through the air and into the water. I take in a few extra gallons and come up coughing.

And there, standing above me, is Viktor with a couple of his buddies. "Hey, you alright?"

I'm still coughing and can't speak.

"Sorry, guess I wasn't watching where I was going."

He reaches out to give me a hand. I take it, grateful to still be on his good side. But when I'm half way up, off balance, he purposely pulls his hand away and watches as I go crashing back in.

When I surface everyone is laughing. I'm embarrassed and pretty angry.

"Sorry, Baptist," he says. "Will you forgive me?" With that he and his buddies stroll off, smirking all the way.

* * *

Now we're lined up on the far wall, guys and girls together, as the coach prepares to read off our names. She's filing through a lot of papers as she tries her best to get the clipboard in order. Everyone's pretty nervous as we stand wrapped in our towels, some of us still dripping. I'm not sure if it's the tension or the slight breeze from an open door, but I can't hold back a little shiver every now and then.

I'm happy that Stenik has decided to stand beside me. It's quite an honor since he was on the team last year and since there are so many older kids he could hang out with. But that's what I mean about him being such a good friend.

As I said before, Stenik's father and uncle both attend our church. But his mother goes to what is called the "Registered" Baptist Church. I know it's pretty hard on Stenik, having his home split like that. You'd think that since we're all Believers we ought to be able to get along better. But we don't.

The Registered Church calls us "pious fanatics." They claim that we're full of spiritual pride and that we're just looking for excuses to suffer for Christ. We say they are compromising the Gospel and accuse them of selling out to the government. In fact we won't even go near their services because we know they are full of informers.

It's not a good situation between us. In fact it's not often a good situation between any of the denominations. Each of us is 100 percent certain that we're the only ones right and all the rest are wrong. It's really kinda sad. Now I don't understand all of the differences, but as best as I can make out, they go something like this:

The Orthodox Christians seem to have the least amount of problems with the government since they've been around for so long and are such a strong part of our past. Like I said, a lot of us think they're mostly caught up in philosophy and traditions and not real faith. But when I think of Babushka, I know that's not always the case.

Anyway, the next easiest group to belong to would probably be the Registered Baptists — like Stenik's mother. Not only are they allowed to meet legally but they can even meet in an assigned building. All they have to do is give the name, address, and work location of each of their baptized members. But, like all the other churches, they can't take their religion outside the walls of their building — you know like evangelism, or helping people, stuff like that. And, of course, when they preach they can't say anything about Israel's place in prophecy. But they can talk about Jesus and some say, with all the new changes in our government, they are even allowed to talk about hell once in a while.

Something else is kinda interesting. There doesn't seem to be a problem for their children to go to their services. Of course, no one, no matter what church they belong to, can have special classes for the kids. In fact, in some places, the government is so strict that parents are afraid to teach their children about God in their own home. And of course no one under 18 is allowed to be baptized. If they are, and the one doing the baptizing is caught, he can be charged a huge fine or shipped off to prison or some psychiatric hospital.

Now there are other groups like the Autonomous Church formed by Joseph Bondarenko, or the Pentecostals, or the Adventists. I wish I knew more about them so I could tell you, but I don't so I can't.

But I do know about us, the Unregistered Baptists.

And I know that everything we do seems to be illegal — from our meetings, to our outside evangelism, to our printing of Bibles and literature, to . . . well, you name it. Papa explains that we don't want to be illegal, that we really don't want to upset the government. But he feels that if we are to really obey Christ in spreading His Word then we have no choice.

I can see Papa's point but sometimes I can see what the others are saying too. I mean, why do we have to be so vocal? Why do we have to run secret printing presses? Why do we have to stand out? I know we have to spread the Gospel but . . . I don't know . . . It's all so confusing. And now with what Galina Ivanovna is saying . . . Sometimes I just wish Jesus would appear to me and say, ''Hey, this is what I want you to do,'' and be done with it.

But He never does.

Now the coach has shuffled her papers for the last time and clears her throat. The room becomes very quiet. She starts off by thanking us for all our ''valiant efforts.'' She explains that whether she reads our names or not, that it's really not that important since the school considers each of us ''members of the team.'' She rambles on with the usual ''collectivist'' phrases about how we all will be at the competitions and how those she selects will only be representing us symbolically, that in reality we all will be swimming, we all will be participating.

This is nothing unusual. Ever since we were seven we've learned to expect these types of speeches. Unlike you in the West, we put our emphasis on the group, not the individual. It's what's best for the group. It's what the group does. It's what the group accomplishes. These are the things that are important. To stand out from the group or the ''Collective'' and draw attention to yourself is considered pretty bad and definitely "anti-social."

So, instead of making heroes and idols as you people do with your Rambos and your Rockys, we honor the group. When a scientist makes an important discovery he has not made it by himself, he has had the help of his group. So it only makes sense that the entire group should be praised. What children do in school reflects upon the teachers and parents so, of course, they also share in the honor . . . or shame. That's why our parents work so hard with us. That's why smarter students are assigned to tutor the slower ones. And that's why our teachers will even help us cheat if it's the only way we can pass.

Instead of "every man for himself" as I'm told your movies say, we say, "The stalk of wheat which stands the tallest is the one that has given up its grain for others."

To me this is one of the things that makes our country so great. Even though it means having to stay awake during these incredibly long speeches . . .

"With that in mind," I finally hear her say, "will the following members please step forward?" Those that have tuned her out, once again start to listen . . .

"Yudin, Polukhin, Lipko, Bashkirov, —"

Viktor and his buddy break into grins as they step out.

"Dmitrieva, Bryusov, Pavlova, Morozov, Ponomarkenko, —"

She's calling the older ones first, the ones that had been on the team last year.

"Semchenko, Kuzmina, Ostrovski . . ."

I throw a glance to Stenik. He nods, making it clear that I shouldn't worry.

"Semchenko, Kuzmina, Ostrovski, Shmit, Kholodenko . . ."

Now she's beginning my age. I notice my shoulders are starting to tighten as I stand, listening. But wait, what about Stepan? Why hasn't he been called? Maybe they've overlooked him. I can't help but sneak another peek over to him. And try as he might I see that he can't hide the look of concern creeping over his face.

She continues to call out the names . . . "Logvinenko, Zaitseva, Kuznetsova . . ."

The kids continue to come forward, from all around us — some that were even in my heat, some that I beat.

"Kondratyuk, Sergeyeva, Yakovlev, Afanasyeva, Vasilievich, Syomin . . ."

Slowly, as fewer and fewer of us remain behind, I see what is happening. I see the truth. So does Stenik.

"Nikitina, Fomin, Shkolina, Yerokhin, Polyanski . . ." She continues reading the names as Stenik and I continue to stand, patiently waiting for her to finish so we can go home.

*　*　*

In the shower Stenik doesn't say a word and I know better than to try and strike up a conversation. Besides, I have my own thoughts. The other kids are pretty happy so I try to look pleasant. After all I don't want to be accused of being a sore loser. But inside I start to feel that numbness growing again.

I turn off the shower and walk across the cold, slick concrete towards my basket. As I step over the shoes to my place on the bench I notice some of the guys getting a little quiet as I pass. It may be my imagination, I'm not sure. But I know I don't want to look up and catch any of their eyes. It's not that I'd break into tears or anything like that. I mean, I couldn't cry now if I had to. It's just, I don't know, I just wish I wasn't here.

Finally I reach the little wire basket that holds my towel and clothes and quickly begin to dry myself. I slip into my shorts and pants and am grateful as I hear the conversations start to pick up again. It's only when I sit on the bench to put on my socks that I realize how tired I am.

By the time I get my coat and scarf on I notice Stenik is nowhere to be found. I look across the room to his bench but his basket is already closed and locked. I think I can understand why. I know he doesn't blame me, he has no reason. But just the same, I figure he'd be happier not to see me for a while.

I close my basket, lock it and give the combination dial a twirl. It has not been the best of days.

Chapter Five

The walk home from school is just as boring as the walk to it.

I only wish Mama didn't know about the tryouts. It's one thing to fail and just go home and forget it happened. But it's a whole other thing to go home and have to talk about it. And you can bet that's what she'll want.

Then, after we've gone over everything in detail, she'll try to comfort me using the phrases I've heard a billion times before. "We must learn to bear persecution — we must consider it an honor to suffer for our Lord — He is our victory, He is our strength . . ." And on and on and on. It's not that I don't believe these things, it's just . . . I tell you, sometimes I just wish she were more like Stenik and would just let things lie.

I mean I believe in God and all. But sometimes, I don't know . . . To be honest sometimes I just want to know why if He loves us so much, why does He let these sort of things happen? It seems to me that if He really wanted people to believe in Him then He'd make it so easy for Christians that everyone would want to become one.

Of course I know what Papa would say. "If the world mistreated God when He came to earth by torturing and crucifying Him what makes you think we should expect any difference?"

But I'm not God.

"Yes," he'd say, "but He wants you to become like Him. He wants to make you 'whole and complete.' "

Then he'd smile warmly, wait a minute, and when he's sure he has your attention he would quote the passage from James he loves so much. I don't know as many verses as I should but this is one Papa made sure I memorized back when I was a little kid: "Consider it all joy, my brethren, when you encounter various trials, knowing that the testing of your faith produces endurance. And let endurance have its perfect result, that you may be perfect and complete, lacking in nothing" (James 1: 2–4, NAS).

According to Papa not only are we expected to put up with trials, but we're actually supposed to be thankful for them . . . "Because," he'd say, "they'll make us, 'perfect and complete, lacking in nothing.' "

I know it probably sounds crazy but Papa sees Jesus as some sort of coach who's down here working with us. He's the coach and we're the runners. It's not that Jesus invents the trials but when they come our way He uses them to build our muscles, (our "faith" muscles Papa calls them) — to make us stronger, more perfect, more whole — to make it so that you and me, so that all of us are "perfect and complete, lacking in nothing."

Now that's all well and good and most of the time I believe it. *Most* of the time. But there are the other times. The times I never talk about. The times I wonder how we can be so right and everyone else so wrong. The times I see that dead, dried-up plant on the teacher's desk. The times I wonder if God is anywhere around or if He's just a fairy tale we've invented.

Of course I never mention this to Papa or Mama. It would really destroy them. Besides, they have enough on their minds. But like I said, these thoughts come sometimes. And today is definitely one of those times.

Now there is this thing with Galina Ivanovna. Could Mama and Papa have missed seeing an answer that was so obvious? Have all of our tough times been for nothing? Why couldn't we pretend to deny God? Why couldn't I take the oath? I could join the Pioneers, finish school, go to the University. Why couldn't I become a famous lawyer or a famous writer? Couldn't I be of more use to God by pretending not to believe in Him? It makes so much sense. Besides, haven't I read somewhere that God doesn't care about outward appearances? It's what's inside a person's heart that He sees? Isn't that what really counts?

As I'm walking I notice that more and more of the people who are passing by have ice cream bars. Every once in a while the market at the corner of the next apartment building gets a shipment. That's probably where the people are coming from. As I get closer I glance inside. Sure enough, the line is already starting to make its way out the door. I look around and see a slow trickle of people from the other apartments heading this way. I think it's safe to say that all Russians love ice cream . . . even in the winter. And since it's still early and since I'm in no particular hurry to get home, I turn and join the growing line.

I'm only a few blocks from our apartment and recognize a lot of the people — people I've known all my life. Not far ahead of me I notice an old Babushka, bundled in her brown scarf and frayed coat. She's bawling out some young mother for not covering her baby's ears.

"Who cares if it's spring," she chides. "It's still too cold to leave his ears unprotected. Do you want them to become infected. Do you want him to lose his hearing?"

This is a pretty common sight; Babushkas are always doing that kind of thing. Like I said, we all kinda watch out for one another. We would never have the millions of people living on the streets and dying of starvation that you in the West have.

It must be very difficult for you to fight and scrape so hard just to survive. It must be frightening having to work all those extra hours just so your rich, capitalistic landlords can keep raising your rents. (Our apartments are owned by the government or by a group of workers from a factory and our rent has not gone up in 25 years.)

And your medicine. How can it be true that if you don't have enough money you will not be treated? How is it possible that if you are poor you could die for lack of medicine? No wonder all you think about is how to make more money than the next person.

Is it a surprise that we know so much about you? It shouldn't be. Every night our TV and radio stations carry news stories about life in the West — like the terrible plague of AIDS you are having as a result of the Pentagon's experimenting in biological warfare. Or your farmers burning all their extra food to deprive the third world countries. Then, of course, there is your exploitation of blacks and minorities — forcing them to live on your streets and in your subways. (Please understand I'm not saying these things to pick on you — all countries have problems they are working through. I'm just saying this to point out how much we learn through our media.)

Of course we don't believe everything we see or hear. When I ask Papa how much we should believe he just smiles and says we must learn to read between the lines. But surely these stories must have some truth.

*   *   *

By the time I get my ice cream it's so soft it's already starting to slide down the stick. It's vanilla, coated with

54

chocolate and nuts. The vanilla is pretty grainy but I've had worse. As I shuffle back outside, past the others standing in line, I'm quickly trying to eat the big chunk that's slipping down the stick. I get most of it — except for the part that splats on the man's shoe.

I try to apologize but it's pretty obvious he's been looking to make a speech about something for weeks. And from the smell of vodka on his breath he's got enough octane to keep him fueled for hours.

"Look at my shoes. Look at my beautiful shoes. They cost me 90 roubles, half a month's wages!"

Again I try to apologize but it's pretty obvious he's on a roll and doesn't want to be disturbed.

"Hooligans. Today's youth, they're all hooligans. They have no respect anymore. No respect. And do you know why?"

"No, why?" one of the people in line asks, just to egg him on. By now he has everyone's attention and they're all waiting with hidden smiles for the show to begin.

"I'll tell you why," he slurs. "It's rock music . . . decadent rock music that the West has smuggled into our beloved country to corrupt our youth. Sure, go ahead and laugh," he shouts to a smirking man, "but when our drug-crazed youth sit in our tanks, unable to defend us from American Imperialist aggression, you'll have another laugh coming."

The smirking man glances to the others, no longer attempting to hide his amusement. As if to answer him, the shouting man removes his right glove, revealing the stump of what used to be a hand. "Where were you when I lost this in Afghanistan? Hm? Hm?"

Suddenly no one is laughing. There's a nervous cough or two but everyone settles down. "We are losing our youth," he shouts. "We are losing them to rock 'n' roll." Somebody tries to gently quiet him but he'll have none of it. "We are losing them to Western clothes — we are losing them to materialism."

He is no longer talking to me. As far as he's concerned I'm no longer there and that's just fine with me. As he continues to shout I slowly step back, drawing as little attention as possible. Then, when no one is watching, I turn and head on down the street.

Alcohol has been a problem in our country for years. With the older ones it's alcohol, with the kids it's drugs. No one's sure why. Some say it's tradition. Others say it's the cold winters. And still others say, unofficially of course, that it's "loss of hope." "What is there to do?" they say. "What hope do we have but to go to work, to come home, to watch TV, and to get drunk?"

I don't know about all this. But I do know I'm grateful to get away before the militia show up. To help curb the drinking problem there are all sorts of new laws. When you can buy vodka and when you can't. Where you can drink and where you can't. And, unfortunately for that man, one of the places it is forbidden to drink is on the streets. Still, since he's a veteran, they may show some mercy.

Already, for the millionth time, my mind is going back to the swimming tryouts. Why wasn't I picked? Was it because I'm a Believer? Was it because of Papa? And what about Stenik? Why didn't he make it? I don't understand, I don't understand any of it. But what else is new? There's so much we never understand. Now it's just a matter of swallowing hard, picking yourself up and moving on. I've done it a hundred times before and I can do it again. I just wish I didn't have to face Mama. She has enough on her mind already.

I hear the crunch of gravel behind me and glance around to see a black car slowly pulling up. I suck my breath in sharply. The KGB drive such cars. Suddenly it scoots ahead and veers sharply to the curb in front of me. The back door flies open and the man from the swimming tryouts appears.

"Nikolai . . . Nikolai Rublenko?" His voice is smooth and harsh at the same time as he steps in front of me forcing me to stop.

I don't say a word. It's safer just to look at him.

"Your father sends his love, Nikolai."

"Papa?" The word escapes before I have a chance to catch it. Then I hear my voice cracking out of control. "Where is he — what have you done with him?"

"Not so fast my friend." He is much more relaxed now. He's in control. He's got me and he knows it. "Your father is in good hands, we are treating him well."

I want to punch him in the gut. I want to throw myself at him with all I've got and hit and hit and hit. But I wait silently, showing no expression. This is a good thing. I can tell he was expecting me to say more, to react more, but I'm gaining control and I'm sure he can see it.

"Tell me, Nikolai. What do you know of the Bibles that are to be smuggled into our country?"

"Bibles?" Again the word slips out before I have a chance to catch it. Bibles? How did he know? How much does he know? What does this have to do with the swimming tryouts? He's caught me off balance again and he knows it. This time he goes in for the kill.

"Yes, by the British gentleman."

He knows. He knows everything. So why is he questioning me? What is he after? The time? The location? My mind is racing. I want to seem helpful, after all they have Papa, but at the same time I sure can't give them information. But at the same time I can't lie. But at the same time . . . everything's a blur. I need more time to think, to put it all together.

"Come, Nikolai, surely a bright boy like you has no interest in a book full of foolish superstitions, hm?"

"If," I hedge, "if it's so foolish . . . why is it of such interest to you?"

I notice the lines around his mouth tighten. "I see." He pauses a minute.

I wait, afraid to breathe.

Finally, he continues. "That's too bad, Nikolai. And to think we were planning on releasing your father today . . ."

I've blown it. I was too disrespectful. I've ruined Papa's chances.

"Pity," he continues, "those cells can be full of such undesirables . . ."

Suddenly something catches his eye. Something or somebody. I want to turn to see but I've already been too rude, I've already made him angry.

Then, out of the blue he seems to change tactics. "Well, no matter," he says, continuing to look past me at whatever caught his attention. "Come with us and we shall take you home."

I feel my stomach tighten. "That's okay," I say, trying to be as polite as possible. "It's just a few blocks, I can—"

But he cuts me off making it clear that he's not asking out of kindness. "It's the least we can do."

For a moment I hesitate, unsure. There are so many stories of people entering cars like these and never being seen again. But what can I do? Run? They'd just be waiting at our apartment. Finally, knowing better, but unable to think of anything else, I duck my head and enter into the back of the car.

I didn't learn till later who it was the man had seen. I didn't know till later that it was Stenik who had rounded the corner and stopped to watch from across the street.

*   *   *

We ride in silence for a few minutes before he finally speaks. His voice is once again a mixture of harsh and smooth. "Too bad about the swim team." He lets it sink in a moment. "And you looked so promising."

Things are much clearer. Now, at least, I understand why I didn't make it. Now, at least, I see the connection.

"Tell me, Nikolai. Do you never grow tired of such treatment? A boy of your skills and intelligence always ending up in last place when you deserve first?"

This hurts but I don't think he can see it.

"You know, with just the tiniest bit of cooperation it wouldn't have to be that way."

There we go. Now I see it. Everyone knows this is how they work. Little "bits of cooperation." It doesn't have to be much. Just a word here or a word there. And it doesn't have to be often. Sometimes a whole year or two will pass before they ask for more "bits of cooperation."

And the rewards will always be the same . . . favors, sometimes lots of them. Sometimes it can be cutting through all the government red tape for a permit, sometimes it can mean getting your children into a better school, and sometimes it can mean not being harassed by the authorities. For a lot of people the temptation is pretty strong, and I can understand why so many are willing to help. I'm beginning to wonder if I understand too well.

"Ah, here we are," he says as we pull up to the apartment. Of course, I'm not surprised he knows where I live.

The car rolls to a stop and I'm more than a little

relieved as I open the door and start to climb out.

"Oh, Nikolai . . ."

Again my stomach tightens as I look back into the car.

"If you ever need our help, for any reason, rest assured that we will be here . . . We will *always* be here."

There's no missing what he's really saying. He's smiling for the first time and I notice how yellow and stained his teeth are. I nod and close the door.

And, as I turn and head towards the apartment, I notice my legs are just the slightest bit rubbery.

Chapter Six

One day Lenin was working in his office at the Kremlin. On his desk beside him was a dried-out piece of cake and a glass of tea.

It was during the period of the awful famine of 1919–1920. Bread was so scarce that it was rationed to only one small piece a day. People ate whatever they could get. Sometimes it would be potato peelings and oats, but that was only if they were lucky.

Of course, Comrade Lenin could have had the best food there was. But he never did. In fact he didn't even take sugar with his tea. How could he live in luxury when his fellow countrymen were starving?

On this day he was working hard in his office and eating breakfast — a breakfast of dried cake and tea without sugar.

Suddenly his secretary pushed open his door and entered.

"You have a visitor," he said. "The Minister of Fishing from Petrograd has just arrived and he must see you immediately."

"Have him come in," Lenin said.

The minister was a simple fisherman, but the Revolution had given him the important job of improving the fishing industry. However, things had been going very badly and today he had come to Lenin to explain why.

"Our boats," he said, "need much mending, and we need new nets otherwise the fish will get away and swim off into British waters."

The man seemed quite nervous as he spoke. Two times Lenin offered him a seat but the man shook his head. He continued to stand — shifting from one foot to the other.

There was a very special reason he was standing. You see, behind his back he was holding a large parcel wrapped in paper. It was a present for Lenin. It was a wonderful smoked fish.

The Minister of Fishing had treated it himself. He brought it all the way from Petrograd to Moscow as a present for Lenin.

Of course, the Minister had wanted to give the fish to Lenin as soon as he entered the office. It was to be a great surprise and that is why he was holding it behind his back.

The man had memorized a small speech that he had planned to say as he handed Lenin the fish. "Here you are Vladimir Ilyich," he wanted to say. "Here is a little smoked fish for your enjoyment. It will do you good."

But the poor fisherman was so nervous that he completely forgot the words, so he decided to stand. He would offer the fish after they were through talking about the boats and nets.

"We will do anything you ask," said Lenin. "If you need more money we will give you more. Only you must promise me you will ease the hunger among our people."

The man was very grateful. He promised Lenin that with this new help they would surely be able to feed the people.

At last it was time for him to go. Summoning up all his courage he finally pulled the fish from behind his back and set it on Lenin's desk saying, "This is for you Vladimir Ilyich. We caught it and smoked it as best we could, and . . ."

But he stopped when he saw that Lenin was no longer smiling. Instead he was scowling.

The Minister was confused. "Please, Vladimir Ilyich, this is for you. I have brought it a long way just for you."

But Lenin continued to frown. Finally he spoke, but quite sharply. "Thank you, Comrade, but I will not accept your gift. How can I when we have children starving in our beloved country. You should not have brought it."

The fisherman was very embarrassed and did not know what to do. So he tried again. "Please Vladimir Ilyich, just try it.

It is very tasty. We caught it in the sea only yesterday.''

But Lenin did not answer. Instead he reached for the buzzer on his desk and pushed it.

''Oh dear,'' the fisherman thought. ''I have made a terrible mistake. I will surely be punished.''

The secretary opened the door. ''Yes?'' he said.

''Our Comrade here has brought us a wonderful smoked fish. He has brought it all the way from Petrograd. Please take it and send it to an orphanage.''

Lenin then turned back to the Minister who was sweating and trembling nervously. But instead of a rebuke or harsh word Lenin offered him his hand.

''Thank you, Comrade,'' he said. ''On behalf of the children, I thank you.''[1]

I close up Pyotr's reader. It took forever for him to finish, but at last we're done. He slips off the sofa bed without a thank you and scampers away to see what other mischief he can get into. Mama's in the kitchen preparing dinner and I can tell by the steam on the windows and the smell of beet juice that we're having borscht again.

I look at Pyotr's book in my hand. There's something so, I don't know, magical, something so powerful about books. I run my fingers over its bent and frayed corners. It's the same reader I used when I was his age. Some of the stories Mama and Papa didn't let me read then and they aren't letting Pyotr read them now — especially those that make fun of Christians or God. But usually the ones about Lenin aren't too bad.

[1] (From *Lenin and the Stove Mender and Other Stories* by Mikhail Zoshchenko, Raduga Publishers, Moscow 1984)

As children we learn about "Uncle Lenin" from our very first day of school. Before that actually, since everywhere we look there is either some statue, or bust, or painting of the balding man with his little beard and mustache.

In kindergarten we had a little area called, "The Red Corner," filled with all sorts of books and drawings about his life. And I bet there isn't a classroom in all of Russia that doesn't have at least one picture of Lenin hanging over it — usually the one where he's staring off into the distance.

Then there are our songs. Songs like:

> "Children live in many nations,
> and everywhere they love Lenin."

Even our grammar books are full of him: "Lenin lived, Lenin lives, Lenin is living."

Of course, when we get older we know that he couldn't have possibly done all these wonderful and terrific things they say. I mean the guy would have to be greater than Jesus or God or somebody. And, in a sense, I guess that's kinda what he's compared to. In fact some Believers accuse the Soviets of worshiping and idolizing Lenin as if he really were God. They say that Karl Marx is their Father, Lenin their Son, and the Communist Party is their Holy Ghost.

Of course the joke for us Believers is that people go to Red Square and wait in line at Lenin's tomb just to see and worship his dead body, while we Believers worship the risen Christ whose tomb is empty.

To say people actually worship Lenin might be an exaggeration. But we do have his birthday off, we still lay flowers at his monuments which are in all our cities, brides still visit his tomb on their wedding day, and we still make oaths that include him. We do all these things and yet, for most of us, it's only for show.

This brings up something very, very important. Something you must know about all Russians. Basically we are two persons . . . the public person and the private person. Each one of us has the public part that says and does and believes all that the Party tells us. And then there is our private part — the part that decides how much of all this we can really take seriously. It can be a very tricky game sometimes — but it is one that we all learn to play. And that is one of the things that makes being a Believer so difficult. Every day we must decide how far to go. I'd like to say that we always refuse to play the game (and maybe for some that's the case), but for most of us that's just not true.

I don't think there's one of us — no matter how good, no matter how saintly — who doesn't slip from time to time. I mean they're not as bad as me — shaking my fist and pretending to yell at God or walking around with my coat buttoned on special holidays so people can't see that I'm not wearing the red scarf. But what about the times they just keep silent? Or try to blend in with the Collective? What about the times they don't stand up and speak out? In their minds it's just as much a sin. I know, I've heard them, I've seen the tears as they quietly confess to each other. There isn't one of us who isn't haunted by memories of denying God. And there's nothing we can do with those memories . . . except live with them.

Mama calls us to the table and I was right, it's borscht. In case you don't know it's kinda like beet soup only some days it's beet soup with cabbage, some days it's beet soup with potatoes, and some days — well, basically it's beet soup with whatever we happen to have.

We sit silently eating our borscht and dark bread which we wash down with a drink Mama has made from some sort of berry syrup. We all feel pretty strange not having Papa there and even Pyotr stays quiet . . . for the most part.

I glance over to Mama and notice how old she looks. The circles under her eyes are much darker and puffier than usual. We'd had our talk. But this time instead of lecturing or sermonizing she simply nodded. Then she kissed me on the forehead and held me a few seconds. She didn't say a word and it was kind of weird just staying in her arms like that. But I figured it was what she needed so I let her do it. Finally she let go . . . but she didn't look at me, she wouldn't look at me. Instead she turned away and said, "Dinner will be in 45 minutes." That was it, that was all she said.

Mama is a strong woman. She's given up a lot and I'm afraid most of it's happened since she met Papa. She was in her final year studying psychology at the University of Moscow, and he was secretly coming into the capital and teaching Bible studies at night. Mama went because she thought it'd be exciting — sneaking off and doing something like that. She had heard of people like Papa, and thought it would be interesting to see what really made them tick.

She had grown up in the Orthodox Church and although her Mother (Babushka) was very devout, neither she nor her Father had ever taken the Gospel seriously . . . until that first night at the study.

She says it was like Papa had suddenly seen inside her, like he knew all of her hurt, her fears, her emptiness. It was like he knew exactly what she was missing inside.

So, here she was in her final year at the University, something she had worked and prepared so hard for.

Already the bribes and gifts were being passed. Already her Father was calling the proper officials to remind them of past favors — anything to make sure she'd get assigned to Moscow or even Leningrad.

This may sound strange but keep in mind that pay or position isn't as important to University students as where they get located. What good does it do you if you make more money than anyone in the world but live in a city where there's nothing to spend it on? In fact, getting a residential permit, letting you live in Moscow or Leningrad, is so important that students have been known to commit suicide if they don't get it.

So here's Mama at the most important point in her life — about to have everything she'd worked and studied for . . . and suddenly she realizes how empty and stupid it all is. How empty *she* is.

Anyway, as Papa kept talking about how Jesus wanted to fill our lives, Mama says it was as if someone had suddenly pulled back a curtain and let the sunlight pour in. Finally she could see what was missing. Finally she could tell why she always felt so cut off, so . . . lonely. The deepest place inside her, where God was supposed to live . . . it was empty.

She kept coming back — four, five times. And after she did some reading on her own she finally asked Papa to baptize her. To this day she smiles when she tells the story. It was a cold January morning, in a heated outdoor swimming pool near the Moscow River. Actually it used to be a famous church until Stalin blew it up and tried building some sort of palace on it. But the new building kept sinking. They tried and tried again but it just kept on sinking until, finally, they gave up and made a swimming pool out of it. Anyway, it was at this site of the ancient church, with the steam rising and the people swimming, that Papa quietly baptized her.

"No trumpets, no angels," she says. But when she came up out of the water there was a cleanness she said she had never felt before. And there was a peace that, according to Mama, has never left her. Even when the hard times come, she claims it's always there.

And I guess the hard times came sooner than she thought. Word spread about what she had done, what she had become. They gave her a chance to deny it, to even admit she had made a mistake and to turn from her "anti-social behavior," but she didn't. So, as a result, she got "sentenced" to our city.

I guess it was this strength that most attracted Papa to her. In any case they fell in love, he was able to get his passport transferred to here, and I guess you got the rest figured out.

*   *   *

So here we sit, eating our borscht in this heavy silence. No one really knowing what to say, no one really wanting to say anything. Then, suddenly, there's a knocking at our door. Immediately our eyes shoot to each other in alarm.

More knocking.

And finally . . .

"Katya?"

Mama's eyes are as big as saucers as she jumps up. "Papa!"

We're also on our feet racing for the door. My heart's pounding. Mama fumbles with the latch before finally getting it unlocked. Then we all practically tackle him shouting, "Papa, Papa . . ."

"It's the strangest thing," he says between hugs and kisses. "They just walked up, unlocked the cell and told me to go. No fines, no job demotion . . ."

"It's a miracle!" Mama's crying. "A miracle!"

Everyone keeps crowding around Papa, but for me the happiness is already starting to wear off. There's something about what Mama is saying. I don't know, it's something about that word. Maybe it is a "miracle," but it seems to me — I mean, wouldn't a greater miracle be if it never happened in the first place? Why do we have to be so quick about giving God all the credit when it was God who got us in all this mess in the first place?

And then there's Galina Ivanovna. Maybe we are torturing ourselves when we really don't have to. Maybe *we* are the ones playing the game — looking for ways to suffer, for ways to let everyone know we're Christians so we can be picked on. Maybe there is a way to believe and still have all the good things. One word to the KGB and I know I'd be on the team, maybe later pass my orals, maybe even get into the University. No one would get hurt. And I could still believe.

I force the thoughts out of my head, feeling lousy that I would even think them. Still, it would all be so simple . . .

Chapter Seven

Sometimes after supper Pyotr and I go down a couple of floors to the Fiakovs to visit and watch TV. Although they're not Christians they are good friends that we've known all our lives. She's a sweet lady with thick fingers and a hairy upper lip. She has a way of knowing more about what's going on around the building than anyone else. He's a joking sort of man with all these folds under his chin and incredible colorless eyes — I mean, it's like they're not even there.

Anyway, they've never had kids of their own so they've kinda adopted us. We don't exactly know why, but Papa says it's because she is Jewish — because she understands what it's like to be persecuted.

She never talks about it, and Papa says we shouldn't pry. But if you ask me, I think maybe she feels kinda guilty about it — I mean that she married a non-Jew and doesn't have to suffer like the rest of her relatives. I don't know. Like I said, she doesn't talk much about it. Except this one time I heard her telling Papa a joke. It was supposed to be funny but I also saw the pain in her eyes. If I can remember, it went something like this:

There was this long line outside the butcher shop one morning because everyone had heard they were getting a shipment of meat that day. But at 9:00 the manager came out and said, "Sorry but we just heard we won't be getting as much meat as we thought. All Jews will have to go home."

So about 15 people have to leave the line.

Then at 2:00 he comes out again and says, "Sorry, we're getting even less meat than we thought. All people who did not fight in the Great Patriotic War (World War II) must go home."

So about half the line goes home.

At 5:00 he comes out and says, "I'm sorry, the shipment still has not arrived and they say we'll be getting even less. All people who are not members of the Party must go home."

So everyone but these two little old men have to leave.

Finally, at 9:00, the manager comes out and says, "I'm sorry, Comrades, but the shipment of meat never came. Maybe tomorrow."

With that, the one old-timer turns to the other and mutters . . . "Those darn Jews — they get all the breaks."

Like I said, I remember her laughing — but it was only with her mouth. Her eyes were definitely not joining in.

Anyway, Aleksandra Fiakov is always knitting something for Pyotr and me, and Mikhail Fiakov is always letting us ride his bicycle, and bringing home pins for our coats. We collect and trade the pins with the other kids, like you do with your baseball cards. Usually they're of Lenin or the cosmonauts or something like that. But lately, we've been seeing more and more on peace — you know, like the dove and stuff.

Because of what Mama does at the textile plant she can sometimes bring home scraps of material to the Fiakovs. Mrs. Fiakov immediately turns it into a dress for herself or a shirt for her husband. And because of Mr. Fiakov's position as assistant manager at a food shop we always know when a shipment of oranges is about to arrive from the south.

That's what I mean about everyone looking out for everyone else. That's how we get along. It's called

"Blat" . . . or "Favors." If you know someone that works at a shoe shop and you work at a bookstore, they'll set aside your size shoe when it comes in if you can get them the latest spy novel.

But it's more than just favors. Once someone knows and trusts you he will give you the shirt off his back. Friends will cry with you. They will laugh with you. In our country once you make a friend you have a friend for life.

That's how it is with Papa and Mikhail Fiakov. Sometimes they will have discussions about the Bible long into the night. Sometimes they will shout, sometimes they will cry — he with his vodka and Papa with his tea. They're as different as night and day, but Papa is sure that sometime soon Mikhail Fiakov will come to know the Lord. I hope so; he's a good man.

Like I said, sometimes Pyotr and I go down there to watch TV. As you've probably guessed, our church is pretty strict and because of that they really frown on anyone going to the cinema or owning a TV. But that's okay because most of us can't afford either.

There are only about two TV shows Papa lets us watch and that's fine since everything else is either boring movies on how we struggled and won the Great Patriotic War, or documentaries about our latest tractors, or scientific discoveries or whatever.

One of the shows we do watch is called, "Come on, Girls!" It's been on for about 18 years and it's pretty neat. They have these girls from all over the country competing against each other — but not in sports or intelligence or anything like that. Instead it's about who can iron a shirt in the shortest time, or who can cook the best chicken, or who does the fastest housecleaning. But when it really gets funny is when these same girls have to rope reindeer or milk cows and stuff like that.

In the end, the one with the most points usually wins a vacuum cleaner or something. And the losers? Well, because of our collective way of thinking the losers get the same thing.

Another show we always watch (Pyotr especially) is called, "Goodnight, Kids." It lasts only 15 minutes and has these little puppets and cartoons. It's kinda nice and always has some sort of message like conforming to the group, doing what's best for your country, trying to fit in and not drawing attention to yourself; you know, good things like that.

But tonight we don't watch TV, we don't even go down to the Fiakovs. Tonight the government has stopped jamming the Christian radio station. They've been doing this more and more lately as a result of their new policy of *glasnost*, or openness.

Maybe you've heard of it — Glasnost. We're all pretty excited about it. Of course some people think it's not going to last, but a lot of others think it's just the beginning of more and more freedom in our country. Who knows? We've had more than our share of hopes destroyed in the past. But, at the same time, this just might be the real thing. I guess, like everything else, we'll just have to wait and see.

Anyway, this radio station broadcasts into our country from outside the border. And when the government is not jamming it we are able to hear programs about the Bible or actual Bible readings themselves. That's what tonight is — a Bible reading.

That means Believers from all over the country are doing exactly what we're doing — sitting around a table and writing down every word they hear, if not for themselves, then for someone who doesn't own a Bible.

I suppose now's the time to say something about Bibles. I mean, we keep hearing all these different versions about how many Bibles you in the West think we have and how many you think we need. Now I'm no expert on the subject but let me tell you what I know.

If you live in the big cities like Leningrad or Moscow there's probably not that much of a shortage. In fact, if you don't own one I imagine you can buy a copy on the black market just about any time you want — if you have the money. My cousin knows a Believer who actually owns three Bibles. Course he's some sort of translator or something but I think you get the picture. What these people really need are study guides and things like that.

But for those of us out here in the smaller cities, Bibles are still pretty scarce. That's why we have to hand-copy them like we're doing tonight.

Every once in a while we hear reports about the government allowing so many thousands to be printed for whatever reason, but we never see them. We figure they're either for the Registered Church, or it's more propaganda, or that they just go right to the black market.

We did hear one report a couple of years back about Romania or Bulgaria or one of those countries down there that let in like 10 or 20 thousand Bibles and then turned right around and recycled them into toilet paper. I don't know about you, but if I were God I'd be pretty mad about someone turning my Holy Word into toilet paper!

"I will extol Thee . . . my God, O King . . ."

Tonight they're going over some of the Psalms.

"And I will bless . . . Thy name . . . forever and ever . . ."

The announcer reads slowly and clearly so that even a beginning writer has time to copy it. And even though the signal drifts in and out, and even though it's filled with a bunch of static, for the most part, it's pretty easy to make out what he's saying.

"Every day . . . I will bless Thee . . ."

Now, there's basically two ways to copy. Sometimes, if you want, you can really concentrate on what's being said and learn from it and almost memorize it. Other times, once you get the hang of it, you can write whatever's being said and not even be paying attention. Of course, everyone frowns on this second way and you usually try not to do it, but if you have a lot on your mind it sometimes happens.

I wish it would happen tonight.

Instead, I hear every word — and every word is like, I don't know, it's like someone is making fun of us . . .

"And I will praise Thy name . . . forever and ever . . ."

It seems so . . . false. It seems so . . . hypocritical.

"Great is the Lord . . . and highly to be praised . . . And His greatness . . . is unsearchable."

Praise God?! For what? For depriving me of the swim team? For causing me to have such a lousy day? For letting people turn His Word into toilet paper?

And what about Papa? We're supposed to praise God for bringing him home. Why? He should never of had to be arrested in the first place! To praise God? How can we — I mean really, if you want to be honest. How can we praise God for all this?

Okay so maybe God isn't exactly the one who does it — but He lets it happen, doesn't He? Or maybe He just forgets about us. Is that it? Maybe we're really on our own and what we really have to do is be looking out for ourselves. And if that's true it makes Galina Ivanovna's case even stronger.

"One generation shall praise Thy works to another."

I feel my throat start to tighten. It's getting harder and harder to concentrate on the page.

". . . and shall declare Thy mighty acts."

I try to swallow the tightness back, but I can't. If God's

not a liar then He's a terrible jokester — playing with us, making fun of us, mocking us.

"On the glorious splendor . . . of Thy majesty . . ."

My ears are getting hot, I start to hear my heart pounding in them. I know I'm not supposed to feel these things and I feel dirty for feeling them. I try to push them out of my head but I'm so angry . . .

". . . and on Thy wonderful works . . ."

I can't sit still any longer. If I don't move I'll explode. I know Mama and Papa have had a rotten day. I know this will only cause them more worry, but I can't sit still any more. I have to move.

I'm up on my feet and crossing as quickly to my room as I can. They may be calling after me, I don't know. Probably. I don't hear. I don't hear anything except the pounding in my ears.

And I don't feel anything except the knot in my throat and the feeling that I have to scream, that I have to shout things I'm not even supposed to be thinking . . . and, of course, the dirty, cut off feeling that comes from even thinking them.

I fling open the curtain separating our room from the other room and throw myself on our bed. Only now do I notice that tears are trying to sneak out of my eyes. I curl up in a little ball hoping to stop the ache in my throat. It hurts, but nothing seems to be able to take it away. My nose is starting to run and I have to sniff it back a few times.

. . . And all the while, in the background, that blasted Psalm continues.

I don't know how long I'm that way. Probably not too long. Finally I hear Papa's voice.

"Kolya . . . Kolya?"

I sit up, quickly brushing the tears out of my eyes. And just in time. When he finally pokes his head into the room I'm pretending to be staring out the window.

"May I come in?"

I nod without looking. Lately he's been asking me for more and more permission to do things. I like that. It's like he's treating me with more and more respect. In fact, he's even starting to ask me what I think about certain things. It's kinda neat — most of the time, but there are the other times — the times I just want to crawl into his lap and be his little boy again.

Anyway, he comes in and sits beside me, but he doesn't say anything. It's almost like he's afraid to intrude. I keep looking out the window. I mean, if he wants to say something then he's got to be the one to say it.

Finally he clears his throat and speaks. "It's been a rough day — for all of us."

He can say that again! I feel that ache in my throat starting to return so, while I can still get something out, I say, "It's not fair — none of it."

Papa just sits there waiting. I have to go on.

"It's not fair we have to eat borscht while others eat meat. It's not fair that we have to be a hundred times better just to be even, that they're always humiliating us, treating us like . . ."

Now I feel the tears wanting to come again. I have to quickly blurt it out before they start . . .

"Papa . . . Papa, they treat us like we're some sort of criminals . . ."

I can't go on. I can only sit there feeling the ache in my throat and trying not to cry. I feel Papa's arm wrap around my shoulders. It's strong. Part of me likes it. Part of me hates it.

Finally, he speaks. But his voice is hoarse and husky sounding. "I know," he says. "I know . . ."

There's another long silence. He starts again. But

instead of going into one of his famous lectures, he talks a lot slower. As if he's trying to put it together, himself.

"Kolya," he says, "our Lord . . . our Lord never promised us things would be fair."

He's not making sense. I turn to him.

"No," he goes on. "I don't think so. When he came from Heaven and died on that cross . . . it was not to make things fair."

He's still talking as much to himself as to me and I still don't understand.

"It was to forgive us our sins, yes; to allow anyone who wants to become friends with God . . . but it was not to make things fair."

It's starting to make a little more sense and he begins talking with a lot more urgency, like it's real important I understand.

"But what we do have, Nikolai . . . that friendship with God, that closeness with the Creator, Himself . . . that's more valuable than any fairness, any honor . . . any riches."

"But why can't we have both!?"

It's Papa's turn not to understand.

I try to explain. "Look at Galina Ivanovna. She goes along with everything the Party tells her; she plays by all the rules, but inside, inside she still believes. And she got to go to the University, she can teach, she can do whatever she wants."

Papa sits there a moment. I can tell he doesn't want to be unkind. He knows she's been through so much — with her brother and all. But he finally speaks — slowly and carefully.

"I'm afraid Galina Ivanovna will not be able to straddle the fence forever."

Again I look at him.

"Nikolai . . . when our Lord died, He died for the

whole man, not just part. When we give Him our life, we are to give Him our whole life. He wants it all.''

He pauses another moment then goes on.

''I'm afraid those who have only given Him half . . . It would be better in the end if they had given Him nothing.''

He wants me to respond, to say something, but I don't. I mean, I understand and everything but if I say I understand he may think I agree. And I don't — not all the way. I mean, look at her, she has it all. How can he say anything would be better? Saying it is one thing, sure, but actually living it, well that's another. And if you ask me, she's living pretty good. After another few seconds he starts to rise.

''Well, I've got some more writing to do. Care to join me?''

I shake my head. No way am I ready to go back into the room and listen to that.

Papa understands and turns to go.

''Papa?''

He stops and looks to me.

I figure all that has happened is because of the Bibles, those stupid Bibles. Papa's arrest, my not making the swim team, the threats by the KGB guy . . .

''The Bibles? Who will be picking them up tomorrow?''

''No one, I'm afraid. The militia are watching us all too carefully.''

Of course, I should have known. All of this and for nothing. Once again suffering and persecution and once again for nothing . . .

Papa leaves and in the background the Psalms continue.

Chapter Eight

It's the next morning now and things are getting pretty much back to normal. Mama's running around trying to fix breakfast, Papa's getting ready for work, I'm waiting for the Semyonova girl to finish up in the bathroom so I can use it . . . and Pyotr's whining about having to wear his hat . . . again.

Pyotr can be such a pain sometimes. Now, don't get me wrong, he's a nice kid and all. But sometimes — sometimes he's just so spoiled. I suppose that's not his fault. I mean, with Mama and Papa losing Natasha who else do they have to baby. I'd mentioned Natasha before but I don't think I ever got around to explaining what happened. It was just a little over a year ago so I still remember the details pretty well.

As far as babies go, Natasha was really neat. But there was this thing wrong with her hip. It was out of place or something like that. Anyway, when she got old enough to stand, she could never really do it on her own — she always had to hang on to a chair or Mama or someone.

And then, when she tried to walk — well that was the other thing she wasn't very good at.

But talk? Man alive could she talk up a storm. And the scary thing was that after a while all the gibberish started to make sense — at least to me.

We got to be pretty good friends those first couple of years. I can't tell you how many times I'd wake up in the morning only to discover she had climbed up on my bed and was staring me right in the face, nose to nose. Then she'd break into that funny laugh of hers and start shouting, "Ko-Ko-Ko-Ko!!" (her word for Kolya). It got to be a real game for her and to tell you the truth I really didn't mind it too much.

Papa was always taking her to the doctors and of course they tried to do whatever they could. But nothing seemed to work.

Then one day, when Mama and Papa weren't home, two men came and started banging on the door. I remember Babushka standing next to it yelling, "What do you want, what do you want?"

They said they were doctors from some clinic and that they were supposed to pick Natasha up for treatment. Babushka hadn't heard of any such arrangement and told them so, but they kept banging on the door and saying they had their orders.

Of course she was kind of scared and confused so she ran over to the phone and tried dialing Papa at work. But the men wouldn't wait. They broke through the door. She put up quite a fight but only managed to get her wrist sprained in the process.

Of course, I tried my best but it was pretty useless. Before we knew it they had grabbed Natasha and were heading for the door. She was crying pretty loud but she still managed to open and close her little fist at me like she did when she said, "bye-bye" — just before she disappeared out the door.

Of course Mama and Papa did everything they could to find her but no one seemed to know anything. Then, two weeks later, we got a phone call from a hospital in Moscow. The voice on the other end said they regretted to inform us that Natasha had died on the operating table.

Mama and Papa were beside themselves and we all

went to Moscow for almost a week, but everyone had the same story. They said Mama and Papa had signed some papers giving them permission to experiment on Natasha so they could try to fix her hip. Papa said that he never had signed any such papers and that the ones they were showing him had nothing to do with what they were talking about.

But it was his word against theirs, so guess who won?

To this day none of us is really sure why it all happened. Of course any time something bad happens it's always easy to say it's because of our faith. I suppose a lot of times that is true and a lot of times it isn't. But Papa doesn't think it's a coincidence that just one week before Natasha was taken, the officials had questioned and beaten him about the location of a secret printing press we had hidden in the woods.

Then there were the parting words from the last official we spoke to. I was standing right beside Papa when they were said and I'll never forget them:

"It's better she die now," he said. "It's better she die now than to grow up in a Christian home . . ."

*　　*　　*

We're on our way to school again — the short way this time. It's one of those gray, drizzly mornings — the type that doesn't get you wet but leaves little misty droplets all over your coat. I suppose I could swing by Babushka's but I really don't know what good it would do. After last night everything's pretty much back to normal. Papa's home, everybody's happy.

Everything's back to normal but me. I just haven't been able to forget what Galina Ivanovna said.

I know what Papa meant about having a foot in both worlds. I mean we're always hearing about compromise, and I suppose a lot of me agrees.

But there's still that other part that says, "Maybe we are a little carried away — maybe we are just a little fanatical. Maybe the films, the lectures, the stories about us . . . maybe they have some truth. I mean how can we be 100 percent right and everyone else 100 percent wrong? Maybe they are right — not completely, of course not, but maybe just a little."

Besides, the Young Pioneers is just a kid's club. It's not like I'm going to stop being a Believer. I know lots of kids from religious homes that belong. I mean, it's not like God's going to send me to hell for joining. It's not like I'm going to deny Him. It's just a matter of being smart about who I let know. It's just like Papa's always saying, "Be as clever as serpents and innocent as doves."

And if I joined, got into the University, became a lawyer or a writer, look at the good I could do . . . for the Lord I mean. It's one thing if Mama and Papa want to stay so strict and unbending. I mean, they're old and they've got nothing to look forward to. But me . . . I've got my whole life ahead of me. Why should I suffer for their mistake?

Another jab of guilt hits me. I feel terrible for thinking this stuff, but my mind just keeps on churning . . .

Pyotr's at the end of the block.

"Come on, Kolya. Hurry, we'll be late! Kolya! Kolya, do you hear me?"

I don't pay any attention. I've got this little switch in the back of my head that I can turn on and not even hear him. It comes in handy every once in a while.

I notice a man wiping off the windows of his parked car with his handkerchief. He's careful not to get any of the muddy water on his topcoat.

Did you know that you can actually get a ticket for having a dirty car in our city? But that's okay, if you can afford a car I suppose you can afford the tickets. Like everything else, cars are hard to come by. My uncle in Moscow has had his name on a list for almost eight years to get one. It's funny, in places like Moscow they've got these super-wide streets, but you hardly ever see that many cars on them.

The man in the topcoat is putting on his windshield wiper blades. Unless it is raining you never see them on cars, and even then you almost never see them on parked cars. When people are finished using them, they lock them away. If they didn't somebody would steal them. Like everything else, wiper blades are hard to come by.

But it's all part of the sacrifice — the sacrifice to keep our country free.

For over 1,000 years armies have tried to invade our country and for over 1,000 years we have had to hold them back . . . almost always by ourselves. It's not been easy. In fact, during the Great Patriotic War we lost nearly one-tenth of our people. In Leningrad when the Nazi's were trying to destroy us, all we had to eat was bread made of sawdust and flour. But we survived.

It's no wonder we are so frightened of you in the West. Not *you*, the people. We like *you*. It's your governments, your military industrial complexes that want to take over. It's their imperialist aggressions that make us so worried.

If you were to see the poster in our history class you would understand better. On our every border are your missiles, your submarines, your jet bombers, your aircraft carriers — all waiting to attack us. We hear over and over again what you did to countries like Vietnam or the

Falkland Islands or Grenada. So, of course, we have to defend ourselves.

The sad part of it is that almost all our money has to go into the military. That's why wiper blades and everything else are so hard to come by. It makes things very difficult on us. But as with all hardships we have our little jokes:

"What's best is for the military —
what's ever left over is for exports —
and all the rest goes to the people."

I hope this will change someday. But until then we sigh, we say our little jokes, and we carry on. We carry on because we love our country. She may have her problems and it may be very difficult to be a Believer, but we love her. We are Russians to our very hearts. We are Russians and will always be Russians.

* * *

It's third period again and I'm heading back into Galina Ivanovna's class. There's a churning and gurgling inside my stomach. I'd like to think it's something I ate but I know better.

I'm moving down the hall listening to a story this guy is telling the others. He's only a year or so older than me but he's already starting to do a lot of drinking and I know he smokes marijuana . . . when he can get it.

Anyway, he's telling this joke about a guy who's all upset with Gorbachev's new anti-drinking laws. The man's been waiting in line forever just to buy one bottle of vodka. Finally he gets so upset he can't stand it and shouts, "I've had it! I can't take any more! I'm going to find a gun and shoot Gorbachev!" But after a while he comes back and gets into line. "So, did you get him?" someone asks. "No," he sighs. "You should have seen the line over there."

We round the corner, laughing, but I stop a little sooner than the other guys, because there, just coming out of Galina Ivanovna's classroom, is the man from the KGB.

Our eyes meet and his face breaks into a grin.

A couple of the kids up ahead glance back to see who he's grinning at.

I try to look away, hoping he'll move on, but he doesn't. He just stays right there in the doorway, smiling.

I know I have to pass by him to get inside so I keep looking down hoping it will help. But it doesn't. In fact it only makes things worse because, as I pass by, he clears his throat and says loud enough for everyone around to hear, "Good day to you, Nikolai Rublenko".

I glance up and squeeze into the room as fast as I can.

Kids are still staring.

He's still smiling.

Chapter Nine

We are all standing around our projects at the back of the room when the bell rings. Normally Galina Ivanovna moves around checking on our progress and making small talk for the first ten to 15 minutes. But not today.

"Class, class, may I have your attention!"

She's sounding very official.

A couple of the guys keep messing around until they catch her look. She's in no mood to ask twice and they settle down in a big hurry.

"As you know, the State Science Fair will be held in our beloved capital next month."

I'm holding Vanya, the rabbit, scratching him behind the ears, but paying very close attention.

"And of course we're all aware of Nikolai Rublenko's outstanding project in Behavior Modification — with his furry little friend, there."

Everyone turns to me and chuckles.

I'm a little embarrassed and don't know what to do with my eyes, so I just look down at Vanya.

"Because of his progress it had been our hope that he would bring the honor of a blue ribbon to our school."

I feel my ears start to warm up a little. I glance up and see a lot of people smiling — especially Vera.

"Now, as many of you know, at this time Nikolai feels he is too superior to join the Young Pioneers."

Suddenly the room is very, very still.

"Which is fine. That is his decision. However, this

same feeling of superiority, this same feeling that he's better than the rest of us, has led him to decide *not* to represent you and me at the Science Fair.''

I shoot a look up to her. She holds my gaze evenly. There's a hardness to her I've never seen. But I can't look away, I can only stare. Why is she doing this? I hear a couple of kids stirring but I don't dare look at them. I already know what they are thinking.

''For reasons we may or may not understand, Nikolai feels he cannot waste his time bringing honor to either ourselves or to our school.''

I keep staring — my mouth is a little open. Why? Why are you lying? Why are you doing this to me?

The kids are starting to murmur — some not too quietly. And for the first time Galina Ivanovna looks away. But not to the class. Instead her eyes dart to the doorway. It's closed. But through the frosted glass there's no missing the shadow of a man — the KGB guy. I see the muscles in her neck tighten as she swallows.

The kids are starting to complain and she finally turns back to them.

''I know, I know. It is a grave disappointment to us all.''

She won't look at me anymore.

''Especially since it will be bringing shame upon the school, giving our splendid reputation in science a black mark. A black mark which we can only erase through extra work and more diligent studies.''

More moaning. I glance to the kids, no one is smiling. Even Vera is frowning — not mad, more like she's puzzled.

I look back to Galina Ivanovna. Her eyes are moving around to the kids, but she will not look at me.

''So, for the rest of the term your work load will be doubled and for many of you—''

The kids are complaining much louder and she has to talk over them.

"I can see no alternative, given our present embarrassment. So, if you will return to your desks and take out your tablets . . ."

Everyone groans or whines or makes some kind of complaint but they all know she means business.

My ears are on fire and my stomach has once again turned into a giant knot. I put Vanya into his cage as quickly as possible so I can get to my desk. A couple of the kids passing are saying, "Way to go Nikolai . . . Nice work Baptist." But I really don't care. All I want to do is get to my seat.

*   *   *

I'm in the lunch line waiting while the cooks in white aprons dump yesterday's leftovers of mashed potatoes and meatballs onto our trays. I glance around. No one from Galina Ivanovna's class is near and that's fine by me. Since she dismissed us I've been moving kinda fast — you know to my locker, the restroom, any place, just so no one comes up to me and says or does something.

I've been trying not to blame Galina Ivanovna. I'm sure she was under a lot of pressure and, in a way, she was only doing her job. I still can't figure out what that KGB guy and her have in common. Maybe he just had word on her brother, but, if you ask me, that seems kinda coincidental.

I don't know if I mentioned it, but a few years back they took her brother off to prison and nobody's seen him since. It had something to do with not taking the military oath. I don't know if everybody in our church believes we shouldn't, but he sure did.

You see, at 18 everyone who does not go into the

University has to serve for two years in the military. It's a law, and it makes pretty good sense. I mean, how else are we going to have an army to protect us?

Like I said before, we're pretty serious about protecting ourselves. Ever since first grade, old timers from the military keep visiting us at school and keep warning us to always be ready. And, of course, we have plenty of civil defense drills — you know, like where we put on gas masks and learn how to survive nuclear attacks.

Later, in ninth and tenth grades, we all take a class a couple of times a week on military things like loading and firing guns, throwing grenades, and lots of other stuff. And for a few weeks in the summer all us boys will go to a military summer camp where we go on long marches, learn to dig bomb shelters, shoot submachine guns, all sorts of neat things.

It's all very important to us so you can see why not taking the oath can be pretty unpopular.

I pick my tray up and look for some place to sit, but except for the tables in the back, everything is pretty full up. I can't help but glance over to the teachers' table. There's Galina Ivanovna, but instead of laughing and talking with the other teachers, she just sits there. She's not even eating. She's got her tray there but all she's doing is slowly pushing the food around her plate.

That makes me feel a little better.

I start moving through the tables as quickly as possible. I'm careful not to look at any faces, and I can feel my shoulders starting to inch up. It's like everybody's staring at me. Of course, they're not, but that's what it feels like.

I'm passing one of the tables when my foot suddenly hits something. I'm falling forward. I try to catch myself but it's too late. I hit the ground but manage to hold up the tray so it doesn't spill all over the place.

I hear everyone laughing and a few start to applaud. I don't look up. I know I've been tripped but I'm not going to make a big deal about who did it. All I want is to collect my juice glass and fork and stuff and sit down some place — any place.

I get back to my feet and search for a table as quickly as possible. I spot Stenik nearby but he won't even look at me. It's kind of weird but I can't think about it right now. Right now I have to find a seat and get out of sight.

I see Vera sitting with a few of her friends at that back-wall table and quickly cross to her — not, of course, without hearing a few expected comments about my coordination from the other kids.

Finally I get there and slip into the seat across from her. But when I glance up, she doesn't say a word. She doesn't even look at me.

The whole table sits there in silence. And then, without speaking to me or any of the others, one of her friends picks up her tray and gets up. Then another. And another.

I watch as they move about looking for a place to sit. Finally, just as silently, Vera rises. I stare at her hoping she'll at least look at me. She doesn't. Instead, she picks up her tray and joins her friends.

I have the table all to myself now. No way do I even want to be here. But worse than staying is having to get up and leave. So I sit and pretend to eat. And as I sit I feel myself getting angry — more and more angry . . .

*   *   *

Three more periods. Three more periods and I'll be able to go home. I want to go now but I've made it this far. I've made it this far and no way am I going to let them force me to run home crying to "Mamochka."

I'm sick and tired of this whole stupid thing. All of it. I don't know what it's all about and I don't care anymore! I'm sick of being the perfect son, the perfect student, the perfect little Christian. No more! I've had it. I'm going to be me. I'm going to do what I want to do — I'm going to do what's best for one person and one person only — me.

I grab my books and slam my locker. I've got my future. I've got my friends. I've got my own life! One of the books slips from my hands and before I have a chance to pick it up someone has kicked it a few feet down the hall. I start towards it but the hall's pretty jammed and before I can reach it they kick it again — and again.

I force my way through the crowd, not even caring who I push. If they get in my way that's their problem. That's my book and books are expensive. I can't tell who's kicking it. Maybe it's more than one person.

The bell rings and as everyone rounds the corner towards the classrooms I catch a glimpse of my book flying in the opposite direction towards the stairs.

I keep pushing my way through the kids and get a couple of pushes back along with a few choice words from the older guys, who make it clear that they don't appreciate being shoved. But, like I said, I really don't care.

By the time I get to the stairs the crowd is already starting to thin out. It takes me a second, but I finally spot the book lying at the bottom of the second flight in a crumpled heap. I slowly move towards it. Once I arrive I just stand there looking at it for a long, long time.

Then, without even knowing it, I realize I'm sitting on the step. The book is just a couple of feet away, but I will not touch it. I only stare . . . It lies there, face down, its back broken, the pages all torn and mutilated.

The lump is in my throat again and I start to feel my eyes burning. I angrily rub at the tears. I can not cry. I will not cry.

Finally, slowly, I reach out to touch the book. I'm very careful, very gentle as I run my hand over its twisted spine, its scuffed cover. It's like, for some reason, I don't know . . . it's like it's me or something. Stupid, I know. It's only a book. But that's how I'm feeling. I pick it up and start to smooth the crumpled pages one by one. I'm going to be late for class, but right now this is something I have to do.

I hear footsteps coming from behind. I don't bother to turn around. If someone's going to say something let them — and let them face the consequences. I don't care how big they may be. I'm in no mood.

But they go right on by. I glance up. It's Stenik. A wave of relief passes through me. A friend — right now my only one.

"Stenik . . ."

He doesn't look at me. He just keeps on moving.

"Stenik?"

Still nothing.

"Stenik, what's wrong?"

Finally, he comes to a stop, and when he turns I feel this incredible chill. He's looking right through me.

"You think we are fools . . . that we do not know?"

"Know what?"

He just turns and continues down the stairs. Then, having a second thought, he changes his mind and turns back. His voice is quivering slightly, but he manages to keep it pretty well under control.

"Suddenly your father is released . . . no punishment, no demotion . . . he's not even fined!"

I'm still searching his eyes trying to find some clue to what he's talking about.

I guess he can see what I'm doing 'cause he finally spits it out. "The Bibles . . . you told them about the Bibles!"

I start to interrupt but he cuts me off.

"I saw you!"

I can only stare.

"He drove you home! And today, today he was nothing but smiles for you in the hall!"

A set up! You hear about it all the time — the government trying to turn us on each other. You hear about it but you never think it's going to happen to you. My mouth is hanging open and I probably look like a fool. I should say something but nothing I say will matter.

"A lot of people would have risked their lives to get those Bibles, but you made sure it would never happen, didn't you?"

Finally I'm able to croak something out. "You think I told them?"

He just looks at me like I already know the answer and how dare I insult him by playing dumb. Then he turns and heads off.

"Stenik . . . Stenik!"

He keeps on walking.

Chapter Ten

WHY ARE YOU DOING THIS TO ME? ANSWER ME!
. . . ANSWER ME!!!!!

I'm outside kicking a bunch of soccer balls into the net.
No one's around. Of course not, they're all at swim
practice!

I kick another ball with all my might.

BAM.

But that's not really what I'm kicking. God knows it
and I know it.

I HATE YOU! DO YOU HEAR ME?? I HATE YOU!!
YOU DON'T CARE. YOU'RE NOT EVEN THERE —
HOW CAN YOU CARE?!

BAM — another soccer ball.

DO YOU LIKE TO SEE US SUFFER?? IS THAT IT??

BAM.

DON'T YOU GET ENOUGH JOLLIES WITH YOUR
WARS, YOUR FAMINES, YOUR EARTHQUAKES?

BAM.

My thoughts are back with Stenik again.

LOVE ONE ANOTHER — SURE. LAY DOWN OUR
LIVES FOR ONE ANOTHER. GIVE ME A BREAK.

BAM.

THEY'RE HYPOCRITES — EVERYONE OF THEM.
MAMA, PAPA . . . THEY'RE ALL THE SAME!

BAM.

LIES — YOU'RE ALL LIES . . . WE'RE ALL LIES!!!!

I don't know how much of this I'm thinking and how
much I'm actually saying out loud. But inside I'm

screaming it. All of it. There's a tightness in my chest. I can barely breathe.

Only a few of the balls have landed in the goal but I'm in no mood to round up the others. As I start towards the net I notice my eyes are burning again. This makes me even more angry. I try to wipe them but this time they won't stop, and before I know it I can't stand anymore. I'm on my knees, hanging onto the net and sobbing like some stupid little baby.

What do you want from me? Tell me! . . . TELL ME!!!

Suddenly I'm not mad anymore, I'm — I don't know, I'm nothing.

"Please," I whisper hoping somehow He'll hear me, somehow He'll make it stop. "Help me . . . I can't . . . please . . . please . . ."

I don't know how long I'm kneeling there, hanging onto the net — my nose running, my eyes running, my body shaking whenever I try to breathe. But finally I start to hear something. At first I can't make it out. I look up. It seems to be coming from the school — from Galina Ivanovna's open window. I look hard and catch just a glimpse of someone or something moving inside.

I start to get up.

There's another crash. And another. It sounds like breaking glass.

I'm moving towards the building now, picking up speed. There's a fear inside me, growing by the second. I reach the double doors, throw them open, and head up the steps, taking them two at a time.

When I reach the top I race down the hall as fast as I can. There's more breaking and crashing. It's definitely coming from Galina Ivanovna's room. The door's wide open and someone's inside.

A couple more seconds and I'm there. It's Viktor! Viktor and a couple of his buddies are throwing and shoving all the different science projects to the floor.

Dimitri, one of the guys, has Vanya's cage on the ground and is jumping on it, crushing it with his weight.

I feel like I'm flying as I leap at him with everything I've got, and we both go crashing to the floor.

I don't know where I'm at — who's on top or who's on the bottom. All I know is I'm slugging him as hard as I can and as fast as I can. He gets a few good punches in too, but I don't even feel them, I don't feel anything — though for just a second I taste something warm and wet around my mouth. I just keep hitting away.

You have to remember I've never hit anyone before — not like this. I mean, I thought enough about it but I've never really actually, you know, done it. And, in a way, I'm really not hitting the guy and everything. It's not really him. It's more like, well like when I was kicking those soccer balls.

Pretty soon I feel these arms around my gut, trying to pull me away. I try to hang on and in the process get a good one, right in my eye — which, of course, makes me let go.

Now the arms have wrapped around mine and are pinning them to my sides as I get hoisted to my feet. I kick and squirm but they've got me tight. It must be Viktor 'cause I'm a good half meter off the ground.

Dimitri is scrambling to his feet and for the first time I get a good look at him. I wish I hadn't. Soccer balls don't bleed. People's faces do.

For some obvious reasons he's not too terribly happy and manages to get a few choice swear words in before he's hauling back and hitting me in the stomach with everything he's got.

The air rushes out of me with kind of an "oofff" sound and I'm suddenly glad I wasn't able to eat much lunch.

Then he starts hitting me in the face. I'm not sure how many times, I'm really not keeping track. Eventually I hear the third guy somewhere from behind shout, "Quick, she's coming!"

All at once Viktor lets go of me and I kinda like crumble to the floor. I can't tell for certain but it sounds like they're heading for the door. I guess Dimitri's still kinda mad, because when he steps over me he can't resist the opportunity to land a good solid kick. By now I can barely see or hear anything so I don't feel much pain. All I know is that the kick has scooted me a good two or three meters across the floor. I must have got him pretty good.

As best I can tell they're out of the room now. But I guess not fast enough 'cause I can hear Galina Ivanovna's voice in the hallway . . .

"Viktor! Dimitri! Viktor, come back here!"

Of course I know they won't, but at least she's seen them. I feel this kinda warm satisfaction and realize I'm trying to smile. I don't know how well I succeed. All I know is that the cold tiles feel good against my hot face. And then I stop feeling or thinking anything.

*   *   *

Now my head's leaning against Galina Ivanovna. I don't know whether I hear her voice first or feel her cool, damp handkerchief, but it doesn't matter. Both are pretty good.

I open my eyes — or at least try to. They're a lot heavier than I remember. And when I finally succeed my reward is this blinding light stabbing into my head. I guess she's turned them on.

"Oh, Kolya . . . Kolya, are you alright?"

I figure that's kind of a stupid question but figure I

should try to answer. When I try, my mouth feels like I just got back from the dentist. I mean I know it's there and everything but I just can't seem to feel it. Then there's the cheek under my left eye. I've never been able to see it before, without looking in the mirror. No problem now.

I start to sit up.

"Kolya — please, don't try—"

But I have to see.

"Please, just lie here and let me—"

I'm already looking around. I wish she hadn't turned on those stupid lights. They're not helping the pounding in my head. Then, after another second, I spot it.

"Kolya . . . what's—"

But she stops. I guess she's seeing what I see: Vanya's cage all bent up and crushed on the floor, but no Vanya. My eyes dart around the room then up to the counter. I barely see something. It looks like his back feet — they're kind of sticking out over the edge.

"Dear God . . .," I hear.

But I don't pay any attention to her. I have to get a better look. I fight to get to my feet. It's a bit of a struggle but I finally make it. Then I kind of half limp, half drag myself to the counter for a better view.

"Dear God . . . Dear God . . ." Her voice is kinda muffled like she's got her mouth covered.

Vanya's stretched flat out, almost like he's sleeping or something. I hesitate a second but finally reach to scratch behind his ears like he likes. He's still warm and cuddly, but he's not breathing.

"Dear God . . ."

*   *   *

The headmaster is the type that, you know, really

enjoys power. He reminds me a lot of those Nazis you always see in the films about the Patriotic War. In fact, a lot of the kids call him "The Gestapo."

His office smells like after-shave. I'm not sure where he got it. It's pretty hard to come by in our town so I figure it's probably a gift, maybe a bribe. Even though there's a few more months before graduation a lot of the students figure it doesn't hurt to start making points.

But, it doesn't matter how he got it, it's pretty obvious he doesn't know how to use it.

". . . and since you were ineligible to attend the Science Fair you stole into the classroom and, for spite, destroyed your project with several others."

My mouth starts to open.

"Oh, I know you say there were other students, but the point is *you* were the one Galina Ivanovna discovered."

I keep staring, amazed at how a man so smart can be so stupid, but he's plowing on ahead as if the last 15 minutes of explanation never happened.

"And since there were no witnesses, I'm afraid that the full responsibility – "

"Galina Ivanovna saw them!" It's pretty rude, jumping in like that, but I figure somebody better set him straight.

His eyes shoot over to her. They are hard and demanding.

"Is that true, Galina Ivanovna?"

There's a pause. I look over to her. Her mouth is clenched tight and I can see the muscles in her jaw tighten and relax, tighten and relax. She tries to swallow and throws a quick glance to me. It only lasts a second but it practically knocks me out of my chair.

It's the same look that was in Papa's eyes!

She's looking to me — a kid — as if I could help. But

what can I do? All she has to do is tell the truth. What's the problem? I don't understand.

Like I said, it only lasts a second. But I saw it and she knows I saw it.

"Galina Ivanovna?"

She's giving that jaw of hers quite a workout. I see her mouth start to open and then close. And then open again. It's like a hooked fish that's been taken out of the water and is trying to breathe.

"Galina Ivanovna — do you know who the boys are?"

She's looking at her hands and swallows again. But I know from experience that she's got nothing to swallow. Finally, she speaks. Her voice is thin and faint — like she's barely there.

"Uh, no, I can't — I can't say for certain . . ."

I can only stare. What? This is Galina Ivanovna, our family friend. This is Galina Ivanovna, the teacher who helped me all year, the person who was always watching out for me, the one who gave me Vanya in the first place . . . I know I should say something, speak up, but I couldn't talk now if my life depended on it. I can only stare.

The headmaster almost sounds relieved. It's like he's back in control again and knows it.

"I thought not."

He looks back to me.

"Because your actions are of such an anti-social and despicable nature, I feel it's important you serve as an example for the rest of the school."

I guess I should brace myself for something bad, but I figure, what's left?

He pauses a minute. I was right; he does enjoy power. "A suspension period of ten days should give you plenty of time to consider your actions."

What do I care. It could be a 100 days. It makes no

difference, not anymore.

Somehow he seems to sense that. Something tells him it's not enough, that he has to go on.

"Then there is the matter of the destroyed property." He clears his throat. "Which, of course, your family will be required to pay for."

My eyes leap to him. He doesn't miss it. The tiniest hint of a smile starts to form around the corners of his mouth. Congratulations, I think. No wonder you're in charge.

*   *   *

The last thing in the world I want to do is go back to the classroom, but I know Vanya's there. And if I don't take care of him one of the custodians or somebody will come in and just throw him away. He deserves better than that. A lot better. Besides, if I went home now Pyotr wouldn't leave me alone until he got all the details. Then when Mama comes home I'd have to explain it all over again. And again when Papa comes home. I'm not looking forward to telling it once, three times would be unbearable. Besides, I know the classroom will be quiet and no one will be there but me and Vanya.

Well, almost no one. When I get there I see Galina Ivanovna sitting at her desk in the dark. I try to back out, but it's too late, she sees me.

"Kolya . . . Kolya?" She's getting to her feet.

We stand there a long moment. I will not look away. Not this time. Finally she starts towards me.

"Please, it is not the way it—"

I can't help it. I take a step back. It's like she makes my stomach sick or something. She's spotted it and slows to a stop, but I don't care. I mean, what did she expect?

"Kolya . . . I had to do that."

I just keep looking at her.

"Don't you see . . . we all have to — one way or the other. It's the only way to survive, to keep going. Don't you see that yet?"

I don't say a word. There's nothing to say.

"Kolya, please . . ."

She takes another step. Again I move back.

Her voice is getting higher, shriller. "You can't fight them. We've tried, all of us. It's no . . ." Suddenly she changes gear. "*I've* tried, believe me, I've tried."

I don't know what she's talking about. What does she mean *she's* tried? Of course she's tried. She's tried and won. She's beat the system, she's got the best of both worlds. But now, now her voice is starting to quiver. "Give it up, Kolya . . . Now, before any more happens to you. Please, Kolya?"

There's that look again. It's like she's pleading, like she's begging. I don't know what she means. I don't know what I'm supposed to say, what I'm supposed to give up.

"Tell them."

She's starting to cry! I can't believe it! I just keep on staring. It's not like I'm repulsed or anything anymore — just confused. And then, finally, finally she blurts it out.

"Tell them where the Bibles are!"

Of course! How could I have been so stupid? That's what all of this is about!

But if she's letting them use her for this . . . if she's become a traitor . . . I feel the revulsion returning. And I guess she senses it too, because she's suddenly shouting:

"IN GOD'S NAME LOOK WHAT YOU ARE DOING TO ME!"

She's glaring at me like she wants to kill me.

I keep on staring. "To you?" I'm thinking. "What are you talking about, I'm not doing a thing. You're the one doing it to yourself. You're the one that's . . ."

"Please, please . . ." Her voice is starting to break. She's not shouting anymore. She's back to the crying. "Please, it's no . . . Tell them, Kolya. Tell them . . . please . . ."

She tries to finish but the words start to get stuck in her throat. She's crying too hard. Instead, she has to lean on the nearest desk, tears streaming down her face, her whole body trembling. She stays there for I don't know how long, trying to stop but unable to. Sobbing. Her nose dripping. She's trying to wipe it away with her hand but it does no good. It just keeps coming — the stuff from her nose, the tears, the emotions.

Suddenly she's looking very small — not like a teacher, let alone a grown up. Instead she looks like one of the primary kids. "Stop it," I'm thinking. "This is not right. You're the winner here. I'm the one that should be crying. What do you have to cry about? You're the one that has everything. You're the one that's beat the system, that has the best of both . . ."

And then it slowly starts to dawn. Could it be? Is this what Papa was talking about? Is this what he meant when he said she couldn't walk the fence forever?

I just keep watching. No matter how hard she tries she can't stop, she can't turn off the tears.

What did he say about compromise? *"I'm afraid that those who have given Him half, it would be better if they gave Him nothing at all?"*

I thought that was just more double-talk. You know, like the millions of things Christians rattle off to each other to make us feel good when we're suffering. But look at her. She's the one that's suffering. I mean I hurt, sure, but not like that . . .

She keeps on sobbing.

Maybe Papa is right. Part of me is a little sad. I mean, I thought maybe I'd found the answer, but look at her. That's no answer. Yes, we suffer. Of course we suffer. But not like this. Inside, I mean deep inside, they can't touch us, they can't hurt us, not like this. Part of me is sad, yes, but most of me is happy. Papa *is* right. Of course he's right. And as I keep on staring at her it's almost like I can feel strength start to come into me — first through my chest, and then my arms. "Of course," I'm thinking. "Of course."

I'm breathing deeper now. It's like this huge weight is slipping off my shoulders, like I was in a pitch-black room and someone finally turned on the lights. It all seems so clear now. How could I have been so stupid?

If Papa were there I would have thrown my arms around him, I would have buried my head into his chest. I probably would have been the one crying, telling him how sorry I am. But he's not, so I don't.

Instead, I look back down to Galina Ivanovna. I don't hate her, not anymore. It's . . . I'm not sure. I guess . . . I guess it's actually pity or something. *"In the end it would be better for those who have only given Him half, it would be better if they had given Him nothing."* Of course. This is what he meant.

I want to reach out, to tell her it's okay. But I know it isn't. I know there's nothing I can do. I know she has to work this out on her own.

I feel I have to do something. What? There's nothing I can do for her, not right now. But what about Mama, Papa? What about all the people I've been feeling so mean towards — like Stenik, people from our church . . . What about God?

I know I don't *have* to do anything, but there's a part

of me that really wants to do something. I can't explain it exactly but it's like . . . I don't know . . . maybe like when you love someone and you know you have to show it — you know you've got to do something. I'm not exactly sure, 'cause I've never been in love or anything but that's probably the closest to what I'm feeling.

Anyway, I keep on standing. I keep on watching Galina Ivanovna. Then, suddenly, almost out of the blue, an idea starts to take hold. At first I think it's stupid and try to put it out of my mind. But it keeps on coming back. And the more I think about it the more and more it makes sense. Finally, I clear my throat.

"Galina Ivanovna . . ." I reach out and gently touch her sleeve. "Galina Ivanovna . . . what time do you have?"

She looks up like she doesn't know where she is.

"What time is it?" I repeat.

She stares at me another moment trying to understand what I'm talking about. I figure there isn't time to explain so I just nod towards the watch on her wrist. After a moment she looks to it and in kind of a hoarse croak says, "4:30."

I try to smile, to do anything to make her feel a little better. "Thank you," I say.

She looks to me — her hair all untidy, her nose red, her eyes all swollen and puffy.

"Thank you." I start to reach out to her sleeve again but stop, remembering that this is something she has to work out on her own. Besides there isn't much time.

I turn and start towards the door, repeating myself one last time, hoping she'll understand what I really mean:

"Thank you . . ."

Chapter Eleven

Now I'm heading down the street, trying not to run, trying not to draw attention to myself, but it's nearly impossible. A couple of times already I've had to force myself to slow down — and I manage to do it . . . for about three seconds. I may be walking on the outside but the inside part of me is running for all I'm worth.

The streets are starting to fill up with people coming home from work and that's good. The more the better. I try to count off in my head how many minutes have gone by since 4:30 — three, five, ten? I can't tell. Now every minute seems like half an hour . . . and half an hour is all I have.

I see everyone — the old people, the young people, anybody that could be KGB, but as best I can tell nobody is watching me. In fact nobody is even bothering to look up. Nobody except a young girl a couple of years older than me. She is coming down the steps of the hospital across the street. She looks kind of pale and her mother is holding her hand. Her eyes are darting all around as if she's afraid someone will recognize her. I figure it's probably her first abortion. She had better get used to it. It won't be her last. Women in my country average six to eight abortions a lifetime.

I round the corner and pretend to head down the last couple of blocks to our apartment. Then, at the last second, I turn and double back. I don't have much time but I have to do this just to make sure no one is following. No one is. After a block I turn and head back towards home. Now, it's true, I could have gone straight to Park Allegiance from the school, but it's too far on foot. In the long run, the Fiakovs' (our neighbors from downstairs) bicycle will be faster.

I can't tell if it's been 10 minutes or 100. All I know is there isn't much time. Once again, I force myself to slow to a walk . . .

Suddenly there's the squeal of tires. I look up just in time to see the black KGB car racing around the corner and heading towards me. I can't see who's inside 'cause of the glare off the windshield, but I can take a pretty good guess.

I spin around and begin running, dodging between different people as the car picks up speed and somebody starts shouting.

I round the corner and immediately crash into a couple of shoppers who have a few choice niceties for me. One has hit the ground and the other is spinning off like some kind of satellite, but I haven't got time to stop.

I've already formed a plan. If I can get them to follow me into the fenced-in alley, and *if* it's locked that'll slow them down by a good minute, maybe two. That's all I need to get the bike and take off. I hear the tires screech again as they come around the corner.

My feet are flying across the cobblestones. It's like the swim tryouts — like riding on Papa's shoulders. I'm not out of breath; I don't feel any pain. I'm breathing hard, yes, but it's the excitement, not the running. It's funny, but in the back of my mind, I know I'm going to win. And even if I don't, somehow I know I'm still going to win. It's weird and for the briefest second I can't help think that this is exactly how Papa would look at it. The realization gives me even more speed.

I cut into the alley. No shoppers now as I dig into the

dirt road and race towards the fence, squinting to see if it's locked. I can't make it out from here. Again I hear the car slide around the corner. They're doing exactly what I'd hoped.

I'm much closer now and straining to see the lock. Still too far. The fence is closed, sure, but that's no promise it'll be locked.

The car is moving faster than I thought. The fence is only 20 meters now but I can hear the car coming from behind. It's going to be close and for a minute I think they've got me. I even catch the car out of the corner of my eye but for only a moment 'cause they have to slam on their brakes to miss the fence.

I see the chain. It's padlocked.

I hit the fence a little harder than I'd planned. Using the chain as my first foothold, I keep scrambling up. I hear their car doors open. My tennis shoes are too wet to get any traction against the slippery mesh so I have to use mostly my arms and hands. I'm nearly to the top when I feel the gate shudder once, as one of the men hits it, and several more times as he jumps up trying to catch my foot. I pull myself over the top and out of reach, but catch my shirt on one of the wires. It rips and gouges in my side. I feel no pain.

I glance down. It's a ten-foot drop but I have no choice. I let go and fall hard to the ground. But again, I feel nothing. If I've hurt anything I figure I won't know it for a while. All I can feel is my heart pounding and my insides wanting to explode.

As I leap to my feet I see the man standing on the other side. He's not two meters away, breathing hard and looking very angry. We don't say a word — we just stand there looking at each other face to face. It only lasts a second but it's pretty scary. I spin around and take off as he races back to his car shouting orders I don't hear.

I head around to the back entrance where they built a playground for the kids in our building and where the Fiakovs sometimes keep their bicycle chained. Fortunately it's there. Unfortunately so is Pyotr.

"Kolya . . . Kolya, what's wrong?"

He's climbing the wrong way up the slide with one of his friends. I ignore him hoping he'll leave me alone. But of course he doesn't. Instead he scampers down and rushes towards me.

I kneel at the bike, dialing off the combination to the padlock as fast as I can. Even though the Fiakovs have said to use the bike whenever we wanted, Papa has given us strict orders to always ask first. But today he'd understand.

I finish the combination and give the lock a tug but it doesn't open. It's probably not the lock's fault, I mean, let's face it, I am a little on the nervous side. I redial it.

"Kolya . . . Kolya! Were you fighting? KOLYA!?"

I'd forgotten about my face but don't bother to answer. The lock clicks open in my hands and I breathe a "thank you" as it drops to the ground.

"Kolya, tell me what's going on. Where are you going? We're not supposed to use the bicycle without –"

"Tell Papa I've gone for the Bibles."

I push off and hop on.

"You're what? Kolya, let me come along! Kolya, wait up . . ."

He's running beside me now as I begin peddling as fast as I can — quickly picking up speed and pulling away from him.

"Kolya. Kolya, I'm telling if you don't let me –"

"Go home, Pyotr!"

"Kolya! Kolya . . ."

* * *

I half-ride, half-slide around the next corner, throwing a lot of gravel on some poor old Babushka. After the scream, I don't hear much more except the word, "hooligan." But that's okay, I can pretty well figure out the rest.

The hill I'm starting up is real steep but the KGB have already checked the front of the building so they're circling around the other way. I have to take advantage of every second by bearing down with all I've got. Unfortunately about half way up, I start to notice my legs.

They're not doing exactly what I want. I mean they're still peddling and everything but not like when I first started. I try to force them down harder but it's like they're getting a mind of their own.

I glance over my shoulder just in time to see the car bounce off the dirt road and onto the street. I'm a good block and a half ahead of them and if it weren't for my legs I'd have no worries, but they're getting slower and slower and slower . . . and there's nothing I can do about them. I take my right hand off the handle bars and start pushing down on my right leg with it, then my left, then my right, trying to force them to go faster. That helps a little but not much.

The car is quickly gaining ground. I keep pushing my legs. The top of the hill is much closer. For the first time I begin to notice my breathing. My lungs are starting to burn. I mean I'm breathing as hard as I can but it's like it's still not enough.

I keep pushing my legs with my right hand, then I switch to my left, but I keep slowing.

Then, it really starts to hit me . . . What am I doing!?

I'm just a kid! These guys are KGB! Who do I think I am? Give up — you're just a boy!

Suddenly, don't ask me why, but suddenly I'm back on that tram with Papa and Pyotr — during that cold January afternoon. Once again I'm playing with his buttons and once again he grabs my hand. That's it, that's all I see. But I understand. I understand why he's been so hard on me all these months. I understand why I can't play the game. And I understand why I can't give up.

My chest is on fire. I feel like I've worn a groove in my throat from breathing so fast and hard. But I'm almost at the top and I keep pushing. I have no choice.

The car sounds much closer but I don't turn around to look. I have three, maybe four pumps to go before I reach the crest. I start counting, like in swimming.

"One . . ."

I hear them shouting. The window must be down and he must be calling to me.

"Two . . ."

"Nikolai . . ."

I see them coming from the side but I won't look.

"One . . ."

The bottom of the hill starts to come into sight and, with it, the bridge.

"Nikolai . . . let us talk, don't be a — "

"Two."

I've crested. I bear down even harder on my legs (which are nothing but rubber) and finally start to pick up speed. The car stays right at my side.

"Nikolai, listen, we do not want to hurt you. There are ways we can work together, ways we can . . ."

But I barely hear him. I try not to hear him. We are moving faster and faster as they stay glued to my side, but I know it won't be for long. My plan isn't finished.

"You are throwing so much away, you are . . ."

There it is, the path! I cut sharply to the left and bounce down the steep, grassy bank. I feel like my teeth are going to rattle out of my head as I hit what must be every bump between me and the gravel walk below. I've got the brakes on hard but it seems to make little difference. Still, somehow I manage to hang on.

Finally I hit the walk, keeping the brakes on until I kind of slide around and begin following it to the park. Just before I shoot through the underpass I throw a glance up to the bridge and catch the KGB guy looking over the rail. Then everything is black. But before my eyes have time to adjust to the darkness of the tunnel, I'm back out in the sunlight.

* * *

I'm riding along the duck pond now, taking it a little easier. My chest isn't burning and my legs are starting to get some feeling back in them. But I'm still moving. Even though it would be impossible for a car to get into the park and even though it will take them several minutes to get here by foot, they'll still be here. I still have to hurry.

There's hardly anybody around and I spot Blackmore almost immediately. Even at this distance I can see he's not a Russian. Maybe he's trying to look too casual, maybe it's the way he's holding the shopping bag, maybe it's just his type of clothing. I don't know, I just hope no one else has noticed.

"Dr. Blackmore?" I hop off the bike and quickly cross to him. He seems a little startled.

"You're . . . Rublenko's boy!"

I nod, still trying to catch my breath.

"Where's your father?"

"He can't make it. They're all being watched, so I've come."

"You?" He looks at me hard — like I'm pulling some sort of prank or something. "You're just a boy."

I feel myself getting a little angry. After all this, I don't need some spoiled Westerner telling me I'm just a kid.

"No . . . no," he's saying. "It's too dangerous. Another time perhaps —"

"Dr. Blackmore, we need —"

"Do you have any idea how dangerous it is?"

Do *I* have any idea? I feel like shouting at him and asking what *he* knows about danger.

"No, I can't have you risking your life."

I have to do something. I can't just hang my head like some kid and let him have his way. I have to say something. And then it comes to me. I speak, but it's not my voice. I mean it is and it isn't.

"When a person gives his life to the Lord, Peter Blackmore, does he not give it all?" I know they are Papa's words and at first I feel a little foolish pretending they are mine. But that only lasts a second because, in a very real way, they are mine. Without even knowing it I feel myself standing a little taller, a little straighter. It's true, they are my words — now they are as much mine as they are his. "When a person gives his life is he not to give it all?"

Blackmore just looks at me. I stand. I'm not embarrassed. I'm not afraid. I've spoken the truth and we both know it. It's not theory, anymore, it's not a bunch of memorized words we're supposed to recite. It's the truth and it's mine. It's a part of me now, it's part of my insides.

Blackmore must know it too. Something changes in his eyes — something softens. We stand another moment saying nothing. Then finally, he reaches out and hands me the shopping bag full of Bibles.

For a second I feel bad for thinking those things about him. He's not spoiled. He's taken just as many risks as me. And in some ways I'm sure this is just as important to him as it is to me.

I try to hold his gaze but the temptation is too great. I have to look down at the bag in my hands. There they are. There must be 20 or so. Deep blue covers, black lettering. I feel the weight in my hands and can't help think about all those hundreds maybe even thousands who are going to be reading them. Some are going to copy them by hand and pass them on. Others are going to cut out chapters and circulate them. And others are going to memorize an entire gospel or two before giving them away.

This is what it's all about — these tiny little books. It seems strange, I mean our government making such a fuss over them. It's like they think they're some sort of powerful weapon or something. I feel myself starting to smile. Maybe they're right. Maybe they are a weapon.

But there's other business to attend to. "You must leave," I say. "They're not far away."

He nods, and I start back towards the bike.

"Rublenko . . . Rublenko . . ."

I stop and turn.

He speaks quietly and softly. "God be with you . . . my Brother."

I can only stand. I have heard that word, "Brother," all my life but never, never directed towards me. Papa, yes. Other respected men in the congregation, of course — but never, never me.

I feel this swelling inside my chest. It's not pride, really, just, I don't know, just a swelling. I don't know what to say. I want to thank him . . . I want to tell him that what he's just said means more to me than he can possibly imagine — that in a way, he's made it all worthwhile. But I can't find the words. I guess I don't need them. The warmness in his eyes seems to tell me he already knows.

I climb on the bike and start back down the path. I'll find a safe place here in the park to hide the Bibles for a day or two. And then, when I'm sure it's safe, I'll come and get them. Of course it won't be easy, but it's not going to be impossible, either. Nothing is impossible — not now.

Epilogue

Stenik and I have closed our lockers and are heading down the hall. School's over for the day and since most of Stenik's friends are on the swim team he and I have been doing more and more things together.

Of course, we've never talked much about that day . . . about how I was set up — about how they tried to get him to turn on me. But that's okay. I mean, we both know what the other is feeling, so why bother?

It's been three weeks now. The Bibles are already starting to be sent out. The authorities have been keeping a close eye on us. In fact they even held house searches in most of our apartments. It was a real nuisance since they go through everything and leave it all a mess when they're done. But they never found the Bibles.

I guess they never thought to check out the Fiakovs, our Jewish friends from downstairs. Mikhail Fiakov says he considers storing them a great honor and Papa thinks he's not only storing them but that he's also been sneaking in a little reading from time to time. I hope so.

Galina Ivanovna hasn't returned to school. They say she is ill and that she probably won't come back for the rest of the year. Mama has visited her a couple of times but doesn't talk much about it.

"Kolya . . . Kolya . . ."

I turn around. It's Vera. For the past few days, ever since I've come back to school, she has been talking more and more to me. A lot of the kids still aren't too friendly but I'm glad she doesn't hold a grudge. The fact that her project was chosen to replace mine probably doesn't hurt.

She arrives, catching her breath. "Listen, I'm having a little trouble with my seeds — you know for the project and all. Anyway they're supposed to be germinating by now and I can't get them to do anything."

I listen, pretending to understand what she's talking about.

"And since, you're so, you know, good at science and everything . . . well maybe, do you think maybe tomorrow we could stay after and look at them or something?"

Out of the corner of my eye I catch Stenik snickering, but I manage to keep a straight face. I mean it's a pretty obvious move on her part but at least the poor girl is still trying.

"Tomorrow?" I ask, my voice sounding a little husky.

"Yeah, if that's not too much bother."

"No!" I realize I sound a little too anxious and try to cover. "Uh, no, I think I can squeeze that in tomorrow."

"Great." She turns and dashes to catch up with her friends. "I'll see you tomorrow, then."

"Right . . ." I call after her. "Tomorrow."

Stenik bursts out laughing and I give him a sharp jab in the gut.

We shuffle along with the rest of the kids until we get outside into the sunshine. It's one of those spring days where it's warm and cool at the same time. I close my eyes and let the sun hit my face as we turn and head for home — the short way.

I haven't gone the long way, I haven't swung by Babushka's since the Bibles. In a way I feel kind of guilty. But in a way I think she understands. It's like, I don't know, it's like she's not that important anymore. I mean I still love her and miss her and everything. But inside . . . inside, I guess maybe I just don't need her so much, anymore.

We cross the street and turn for home when my stomach suddenly knots up into that tight, sick feeling. There, standing next to his car, is the KGB guy. And there's no question who he's waiting for.

"Hello, Nikolai."

He smiles as we come closer. I don't want to stop but I know we don't have much choice.

"How are you feeling?"

I nod an okay.

"Good, good." He finishes his cigarette then drops it to the ground and smashes it out. "We just wanted to drop by and say, 'hello' . . . and to assure you that we'll be staying in touch from time to time."

We wait in silence for him to continue. He takes a slow breath and then pretends to yawn. "How does the old saying go . . . 'The battle may be won, but the war is not over'? "

He smiles. His teeth look particularly yellow in the bright sun.

"We'll be keeping a close eye on you my friend. You will not be forgotten."

We continue to stand, not sure what to do, and then I hear:

"Kolya . . ."

It's Pyotr. A deep chill goes through me.

"Kolya . . ."

I spin around, trying to motion for him to stay away, to go back. But it's too late, he's nearly reached us — and with so many books he can barely see over the top of them.

"Why don't you ever wait up for me? You know what Mama said about — "

I'm furious. Can't he see who this man is — can't he

see how dangerous it is? Can't he shut up for just a second? I mean if there was any doubt in this guy's mind that Pyotr was my brother, there certainly isn't now.

When I glance back to the man he doesn't seem to show much recognition. And even if he does it's pretty obvious he doesn't really care.

A wave of relief passes over me.

I don't know what to do so I try to play it as nonchalantly as possible. "Why aren't you ever on time?" I pretend to taunt, as I remove just enough books to see his beady little eyes. But, before I can signal him what's going on, I notice the KGB guy start to turn and get back into his car. Stenik and I exchange glances.

"You know you get out earlier than me!" Pyotr whines.

The car starts up and, after a moment, it slowly pulls away. Stenik and I don't say a word.

"Kolya . . ."

I continue to watch until it finally turns the corner and disappears out of sight.

"KOLYA . . ."

"Pyotr . . . do you always have to be such a pain . . . I mean *always*!"

"What?"

I turn and start back towards home with Stenik.

"You take that back!"

He's trying to follow but the books make it pretty tough to keep up.

"I would if it weren't the truth."

"Kolya . . . I'm telling . . . Kolya, if you don't take that back, I'm—"

I hear a couple of books drop to the ground — and then more.

"Kolya . . ."

I motion to Stenik to slow up a little, but, hopefully, not enough for Pyotr to notice. Then, almost against my will, I feel myself starting to break into a sad little smile. Not because of Pyotr's struggle with the books. I mean if he really needed me I'd be there — I'll always be there. I guess I'm just smiling because . . . I'm not sure. I guess because I know he won't be this way forever. And, to be honest, I guess I'll be a little sad when he changes — a "*little*."

"Kolya . . ."

But, I guess we all have to grow up . . . sometime or another.

"Kolya . . ."

Yes, I think, in one way or another we all have to grow up.

Open Doors News Brief

(U.S. and Canada Only)

If you would like to know more about Open Doors with Brother Andrew and its ministry to the Suffering Church, write to the address below. We'll send you a free six-month subscription to the *Open Doors News Brief*. This monthly publication will bring you timely news and information about persecuted Christians around the world.

Open Doors with Brother Andrew
P.O. Box 27001
Santa Ana, CA 92799
United States

P.O. Box 597
Streetsville, ON L5M 2C1
Canada

If you live outside the U.S. or Canada and would like more information, write to the Open Doors office nearest you:

Australia
P.O. Box 53 – Seaforth, NSW – Australia 2092

England
P.O. Box 6 – Standlake, Witney –
Oxon OX8 7SP – England

The Netherlands
P.O. Box 47 – 3850AA Ermelo – The Netherlands

New Zealand
P.O. Box 6123 – Auckland 1 – New Zealand

Singapore
1 Sophia Road – # 03-28, Peace Centre –
Singapore 0922

South Africa
P.O. Box 990099 – Kibler Park –
2053 Johannesburg – S. Africa